YORK NOTES

MACBETH

WILLIAM SHAKESPEARE

Notes by Alasdair D. F. Macrae
Revised by Keith West

Longman
is an imprint of

PEARSON

York Press

The right of Alasdair D. F. Macrae to be identified as the Author of this Work has been asserted
by him in accordance with the Copyright, Designs and Patents Act 1988

YORK PRESS
322 Old Brompton Road, London SW5 9JH

PEARSON EDUCATION LIMITED
Edinburgh Gate, Harlow,
Essex CM20 2JE, United Kingdom

Associated companies, branches and representatives throughout the world

First published 2001
New edition 2005
This new and fully revised edition 2012

10 9 8 7 6 5 4 3 2 1

ISBN 978–1–4479–1314–6

Illustration on p. 9 by Neil Gower
Phototypeset by Carnegie Book Production
Printed in Slovakia by Neografia

Photo Credits
© INTERFOTO/Alamy for page 6 / Ryan Jorgensen//Jorgo/Shutterstock.com for page 7 /
© Robert Stainforth/Alamy for page 8 / © iStockphoto.com/Jamesmcq24 for page 10 / Vasiliy
Koval/Shutterstock.com for page 11 / Elenamiv/Shutterstock.com for page 12 / Krasowit/
Shutterstock.com for page 14 / Elnur/Shutterstock.com for page 15 / © iStockphoto.com/
RonTech2000 for page 16 / Csaba Peterdi/Shutterstock.com for page 17 / © iStockphoto.com/
QUAYSIDE for page 18 / Elnur/Shutterstock.com for page 19 / Eric Isselée/Shutterstock.com for
page 20 / stenic56/Shutterstock.com for page 21 / © iStockphoto.com/talymel for page 22 /
© iStockphoto.com/ivstiv for page 24 / © iStockphoto.com/jimkruger for page 25 /
© iStockphoto.com/Andy445 for page 26 / Denis Kukareko/Shutterstock.com for page 27 /
© iStockphoto.com/klenger for page 28 / © iStockphoto.com/sharply_done for page 29 /
© iStockphoto.com/M-Reinhardt for page 30 / © iStockphoto.com/talymel for page 31 /
© iStockphoto.com/YsaL for page 32 / Brocorwin/Shutterstock.com for page 33 / © iStockphoto.
com/Pshenichka for page 35 / DSBfoto/Shutterstock.com for page 36 / marco mayer/
Shutterstock.com for page 37 / llaszlo/Shutterstock.com for page 38 / trucic/Shutterstock.com
for page 39 / Marcin Ciesielski/Sylwia Cisek/Shutterstock.com for page 45 / Alexander
Lobanov/Shutterstock.com for page 46 / Masson/Shutterstock.com for page 48 / © iStockphoto.
com/kkgas for page 51 / © iStockphoto.com/duncan1890 for page 52 / © iStockphoto.com/
talymel for page 54 / © iStockphoto.com/Bliznetsov for page 55 / © iStockphoto.com/
lynnwoodward for page 56 / Dm_Cherry/Shutterstock.com for page 57 / © iStockphoto.com/
ManuelVelasco for page 58 / © iStockphoto.com/Inkout for page 59 / GekaSkr/Shutterstock.
com for page 60 / Dmitry Naumov/Shutterstock.com for page 62 / © iStockphoto.com/LdF for
page 63 / nadirco/Shutterstock.com for page 67 / © iStockphoto.com/johnaudrey for page 69 /
mihalec/Shutterstock.com for page 70 / © iStockphoto.com/kutaytanir for page 71 / Rafael
Ramirez Lee/Shutterstock.com for page 72 / R-photos/Shutterstock.com for page 73 / Lance
Bellers/Shutterstock.com for page 75 / © iStockphoto.com/ecliff6 for page 76 top /
© iStockphoto.com/Lovattpics for page 76 bottom / © The Print Collector/Alamy for page 77 /
© iStockphoto.com/spooh for page 78 / Baloncici/Shutterstock.com for page 79 / © iStockphoto.
com/Goldfaery for page 92 / © iStockphoto.com/skynesher for page 95

CONTENTS

PART FIVE: CONTEXTS AND CRITICAL DEBATES

PART SIX: GRADE BOOSTER

ESSENTIAL STUDY TOOLS

PART ONE: INTRODUCING *MACBETH*

HOW TO STUDY *MACBETH*

These Notes can be used in a range of ways to help you read, study and (where relevant) revise for your exam or assessment.

READING THE PLAY

Read the play once, fairly quickly, for pleasure. This will give you a good sense of the over-arching shape of the plot, and a good feel for the highs and lows of the action, the pace and style, and the sequence in which information is withheld or revealed. You could ask yourself:

- How do individual characters change or develop? How do my own responses to them change?
- How does Shakespeare allow the audience to see into the minds and motives of the characters? Does he use **asides**, **soliloquies** or other dramatic devices, for example?
- What sort of language do different characters use? Does Shakespeare use **imagery**, or recurring motifs or symbols?
- Are the events presented chronologically, or is the time scheme altered in some way?
- What impressions do the locations and settings, such as the heath, make on my reading and response to the play?
- How could the play be presented on the stage in different ways? How could different types of performance affect the audience's interpretation of the play?

On your second reading, make detailed notes around the key areas highlighted above and in the Assessment Objectives, such as form, language, structure (AO2), links and connections to other texts (AO3) and the context/background for the play (AO4). These may seem quite demanding, but these Notes will suggest particular elements to explore or jot down.

INTERPRETING OR CRITIQUING THE PLAY

Although it's not helpful to think in terms of the play being 'good' or 'bad', you should consider the different ways the play can be read. How have critics responded to it? Do their views match yours – or do you take a different viewpoint? Are there different ways you can interpret specific events, characters or settings? This is a key aspect in AO3, and it can be helpful to keep a log of your responses and the various perspectives which are expressed both by established critics and by classmates, your teacher, or other readers.

REFERENCES AND SOURCES

You will be expected to draw on critics' or reviewers' comments, and to refer to relevant literary or historical sources that might have influenced Shakespeare or his contemporaries. Make sure you keep accurate, clear notes of writers or sources you have used – for example, noting down titles of works, authors' names, website addresses, dates, etc. You may not have to reference all these things when you respond to a text, but knowing the source of your information will allow you to go back to it, if need be – and to check its accuracy and relevance.

REVISING FOR AND RESPONDING TO AN ASSESSED TASK OR EXAM QUESTION

The structure and the contents of these Notes are designed to help give you the relevant information or ideas needed to answer tasks you have been set. First, work out the key words or ideas from the task (for example, 'form', 'Act I', 'Duncan'), then read the relevant parts of the Notes that relate to these terms or words, selecting what is useful for revision or written response. Then, turn to **Part Six: Grade Booster** for help in formulating your actual response.

> **GRADE BOOSTER** (A01)
>
> Remember: most of us need to read Shakespeare's plays many times for a complete understanding. *Macbeth* is no exception. You might need to revisit key passages quite often until you have gained a balanced understanding to aid your interpretation of the play as a whole.

MACBETH IN CONTEXT

1564	William Shakespeare born in Stratford-upon-Avon.
1582	Shakespeare marries Anne Hathaway. Outbreak of the plague in London.
1592	Shakespeare writes *The Comedy of Errors* and Christopher Marlowe writes *Doctor Faustus*. London theatres close due to an outbreak of the plague.
1596	Shakespeare's son, Hamnet, dies.
1597	James VI of Scotland (later James I of England) writes *Demonology*.
1603	James VI of Scotland becomes James I of England.
1606	Shakespeare writes *Macbeth*.
1612	Shakespeare retires and returns to Stratford-upon-Avon. The last burning of heretics in England takes place.
1613	Shakespeare writes *Henry VIII*. The Globe theatre burns down.
1616	Shakespeare dies.

SHAKESPEARE'S THEATRE

Full-length plays, adopting the devices of classical drama and offering a range of characterisation, were not attempted in English drama before the Renaissance. From the late 16th century onwards, men such as Christopher Marlowe and Thomas Kyd began to write full-length plays for performance. James Burbage built the first permanent theatre in England in 1576 and more theatres were soon to follow. By the time Shakespeare arrived in London, there were full-length plays, theatres and acting companies, and he soon found himself involved in acting and writing plays.

CHECK THE BOOK A03

Film producers can offer a visual approach to the bleak landscapes in this play. *Interpreting Shakespeare on Screen* (2000) by Deborah Cartmell offers a clear examination of ways to approach Shakespeare through cinematic versions of his plays.

EARLY STAGING

We know for certain that *Macbeth* was performed in 1611 because a very full eyewitness account survives. All the evidence available to us suggests that *Macbeth* was first performed in 1606, possibly in front of King James I himself. The play was seriously altered in 1663 to bring it more into line with the tastes of the period and this rather operatic version with songs and dances survived into the nineteenth century. Most modern productions use Sharkespeare's original text.

SETTING

Macbeth is set in Scotland – with just one scene set in the King's Palace in England (IV.3). Much of the action takes place in three areas – on a bleak heath, a camp near a battlefield and in or around various castles. One exception is the Witches' meeting with Hecat at the Pit of Acheron (Hell). The settings present us with a bleak and **Gothic** feel to the play. Even inside the palace, with Macbeth as king, there are plots and whisperings of murders. The park, outside the palace, is set in the dark – this is where Banquo is murdered.

Whenever the Witches appear there is a thunderstorm and the landscape is bleak and uninviting.

KEY ISSUES

Macbeth is probably the most widely read and seen of William Shakespeare's plays. It is one of his shortest plays and has focus and succinctness which fit an uncluttered plot. It highlights what seem to be straightforward moral dilemmas. Although the story is set in a specific historical period and place, the themes are of universal interest and relevance. Themes such as ambition, loyalty, social and psychological order and the struggle of good and evil deal with what is ultimately valuable in human life. The story itself has a clear shape with distinct stages and a firm ending; there are fights, murders, witches, ghosts and nightmares among its sensational ingredients. With very few main characters and no subplot, it is easily held in the mind of the reader.

GOTHIC ELEMENTS

Although the play *Macbeth* predates the Gothic genre, there are elements in *Macbeth* that are distinctly Gothic. The settings (see above) are generally dark and claustrophobic, and fear, guilt and the sightings of ghosts are all aspects of the genre. Macbeth (III.4) is disturbed and frightened by his vision of the murdered Banquo – this scene in particular brings together five elements of the Gothic genre in fear, guilt, murder, blood and a ghost. The setting, inside a castle, is also Gothic. A castle is often used as a Gothic backdrop – possibly because the first Gothic novel, *The Castle of Otranto*, was set in a bleak castle.

The supernatural – the witches, the dagger and a ghost – also provides important evidence of Gothic in the play. Lady Macbeth conjures evil and asks to be unnaturally unsexed (I.5). After the murder of Duncan, the very night acts against nature as horses are said to have eaten each other (II.4) and a falcon is reported to have been killed by a much smaller bird. Much of the play takes place in darkness or half-light, adding mystery and uncertainty to events. Lady Macbeth's madness and the emphasis on blood – 'Who would have thought the old man to have so much blood in him?' (V.1.39–40) – are also features of the genre, as physical and mental torment are used to heighten the action.

MACBETH IN PERFORMANCE

The play is memorable and easily adapted. This has resulted in it being produced in innumerable versions across the world. Verdi's *Macbeth* is a favourite in the opera repertoire; and some of the more famous films based on the play include the Hollywood gangster movie *Joe Macbeth* (1955) set in Chicago with a gangland climax, and *Throne of Blood* (1957), by the Japanese director Akira Kurosawa, set in a medieval Japan of warlords engaged in a struggle for domination.

It is good advice to see a theatre production of *Macbeth* but remember, the production will be interpreted by the director and the cast. Nevertheless, a live production is how Shakespeare intended us to view his play. He had no idea that we would study the play text, analyse the characters and write about the play for an extended piece of work or for

---

CONTEXT **A04**

In British theatres, *Macbeth* has, for all its popularity, come to be associated with a superstition of bad luck, and actors and stage workers avoid referring to the play by its name when it is in production. It is often referred to as 'The Scottish Play'.

CONTEXT **A04**

The first Gothic novel was written by the politician Horace Walpole in 1764. *The Castle of Otranto* contains all the elements that have come to be associated with the genre, from conspiracy and suspense to supernatural events and murder, and like *Macbeth*, contains a prophecy that affects future events.

an examination. He wanted us to see it – so the visual aspects of the play are important. Seeing a production means that we can carry the images with us as we study the play. Through the performances of experienced actors, the language will come to life and you will understand the flow of the speeches. There are a number of good productions worth watching and comparing. For example, Roman Polanski's *Macbeth* (1971) has stood the test of time and there have been a number of BBC productions, too. One of the latest film versions of *Macbeth* is Geoffrey Wright's production – which is a contemporary retelling and is set in the ganglands of Melbourne, Australia. The theatre and film versions must be complementary to your reading of the play – and are never a substitute.

GRADE BOOSTER **A02**

When studying the play, think about how the characters relate to each other. What motivates the main characters? For example, what motivates Lady Macbeth?

LINE OF SUCCESSION

Both Macbeth and Duncan existed in real life, and both were kings of Scotland. The play is based on events that are real but Shakespeare changed the characters' behaviour to suit his own ideas. Contrary to the play, history suggests that Duncan was a weak king while Macbeth was a respected ruler.

As the line of succession diagram below indicates, Duncan and Macbeth were cousins through their mother's line. Malcolm II had died leaving daughters (Bethoc and Donada) but no son, so, as women were not allowed to rule, the crown skipped a generation and passed to his grandson Duncan I.

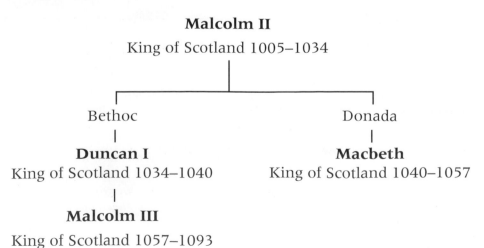

Malcolm II
King of Scotland 1005–1034

Bethoc   Donada

Duncan I   **Macbeth**
King of Scotland 1034–1040   King of Scotland 1040–1057

Malcolm III
King of Scotland 1057–1093

CHARACTERS IN *MACBETH*

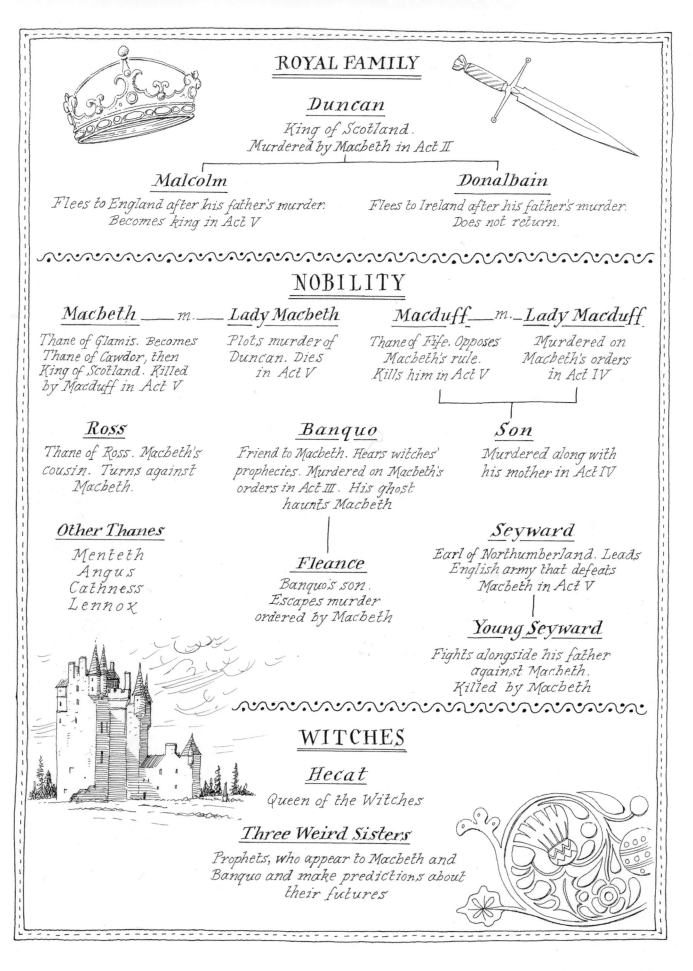

ROYAL FAMILY

Duncan
King of Scotland.
Murdered by Macbeth in Act II

Malcolm
Flees to England after his father's murder.
Becomes king in Act V

Donalbain
Flees to Ireland after his father's murder.
Does not return.

NOBILITY

Macbeth — m. — **Lady Macbeth**

Macbeth
Thane of Glamis. Becomes
Thane of Cawdor, then
King of Scotland. Killed
by Macduff in Act V

Lady Macbeth
Plots murder of
Duncan. Dies
in Act V

Macduff — m. — **Lady Macduff**

Macduff
Thane of Fife. Opposes
Macbeth's rule.
Kills him in Act V

Lady Macduff
Murdered on
Macbeth's orders
in Act IV

Ross
Thane of Ross. Macbeth's
cousin. Turns against
Macbeth.

Banquo
Friend to Macbeth. Hears witches'
prophecies. Murdered on Macbeth's
orders in Act III. His ghost
haunts Macbeth

Son
Murdered along with
his mother in Act IV

Other Thanes
Menteth
Angus
Cathness
Lennox

Fleance
Banquo's son.
Escapes murder
ordered by Macbeth

Seyward
Earl of Northumberland. Leads
English army that defeats
Macbeth in Act V

Young Seyward
Fights alongside his father
against Macbeth.
Killed by Macbeth

WITCHES

Hecat
Queen of the Witches

Three Weird Sisters
Prophets, who appear to Macbeth and
Banquo and make predictions about
their futures

SYNOPSIS

REBELLION

Three witches meet on a heath in bad weather. There is thunder and lightning. They plan to meet Macbeth after the battle between the rebels and King Duncan's forces.

The authority of Duncan, King of Scotland, is under threat from rebellions by some of his nobles and attacks by invading Vikings. A wounded captain reports that Macbeth, Thane of Glamis, is the fiercest warrior in support of King Duncan. Macbeth has defeated the rebellious Highlanders who were led by Macdonwald (pronounced Macdonald). As soon as the Highlanders were defeated, the opportunist King of Norway attacked the tired Scottish army. Macbeth and Banquo led their men to defeat the Norwegian army. Macbeth is rewarded with an added title, Thane of Cawdor, the former Thane of Cawdor having been executed for treachery as one of the rebels.

THE WITCHES

The three Witches meet Macbeth and Banquo on the heath. The two men are returning from battle and are due to meet King Duncan at Forres.

The Witches immediately invoke the influence of the supernatural. They appear to be able to anticipate events before they actually happen. Each of the three Witches greets Macbeth differently. They lead Macbeth and Banquo to believe that greater honours lie ahead for them – in Macbeth's case the crown of Scotland, in Banquo's that his sons will be kings. Macbeth takes their predictions very seriously and writes to his wife, Lady Macbeth.

THE MURDER

When Duncan comes to spend the night with Macbeth in his castle, Lady Macbeth urges her husband to seize the opportunity to murder the king. She has previously asked for evil spirits to enter her body so that she loses her femininity and can persuade Macbeth to undertake this deed.

Despite being a fierce soldier, Macbeth is reluctant to kill the sleeping king, who is under his protection as a host. It is a very nervous Macbeth who kills Duncan and he immediately regrets his action. Lady Macbeth is forced to complete the job by placing the blood-covered daggers beside Duncan's servants and smearing the servants with blood. During the night nature rebels, suggesting that God and nature are against the murder of the king.

DISCOVERING THE MURDER

When the king's murdered body is discovered by Macduff in the early morning, Macbeth attempts to cover his tracks by murdering the servants, claiming he acted in a fit of righteous outrage. Duncan's sons, Malcolm and Donalbain, guessing that somebody might implicate them in their father's murder, flee in fear for their lives. Malcolm goes to England and Donalbain to Ireland. Macbeth is crowned as the new king.

FURTHER MURDERS

Because the Witches have predicted Banquo's offspring will become kings, Macbeth decides to have Banquo and his only son, Fleance, murdered. Banquo is killed but Fleance escapes. At a banquet, hosted by the new king and queen, Macbeth receives news of Banquo's death. He also hears that Fleance has escaped and knows the Witches' predictions might still come true. As he returns to the table, he cannot find a spare seat. Banquo's ghost appears to Macbeth and he is terrified. Although the banquet is disrupted, Lady Macbeth is able, in part, to cover for him. She informs the guests that he has suffered a type of illness from his youth.

MACBETH'S MORAL DESCENT

In Scotland rumours of plots and conspiracies abound. There is a general sense of corruption and fear. Macbeth seeks out the Witches but receives very unclear, ambiguous messages from them. The unclear messages encourage his suspicious nature. He is told to beware the Thane of Fife, but his fears are then calmed when he hears that no one born of a woman can harm him and that he will only be defeated when Birnam Wood comes to Dunsinane, an event that he believes to be impossible. When he hears that Macduff, Thane of Fife, has left Scotland, he suspects a conspiracy is plotted against him. Macduff has gone to England to seek help from the English king. In a fit of anger, Macbeth orders Macduff's wife and children to be murdered. Macduff receives news of their death while he is in discussion at the English court. He is devastated and unable to understand that his wife and all his children are dead. He is with Malcolm, Duncan's exiled son. Malcolm consoles Macduff in his grief and urges him to think of revenge against Macbeth. They agree to lead an army against the usurper.

A FINAL BATTLE

Back in Scotland, Lady Macbeth's mental stability has collapsed due to her guilt. She is prone to sleep walking and uttering thoughts that are dangerous for anyone to hear. She speaks about the deaths of Duncan, Lady Macduff and also Banquo. The doctor fears for Lady Macbeth's life.

Macbeth is deserted by many of his previous supporters. As his castle in Dunsinane comes under attack, he is told of his wife's suicide. He is now virtually alone and bravely stands against his attackers. He reflects on the insignificance of his life. Later, as Macbeth is told that Birnam Wood is moving towards Dunsinane, he realises the Witches have tricked him into a false sense of security. During the battle, Macbeth kills Young Seyward and discovers that his castle has been taken. Macduff finally manages to find Macbeth and points out the folly of the Witches' predictions. Macbeth is disheartened as he realises the faith he placed in the Witches was a false hope. However, he will not yield and watch Malcolm crowned as king. Macbeth fights Macduff, but is killed. Malcolm is declared King of Scotland, in front of Macbeth's severed head. Order is restored to Scotland.

CHECK THE BOOK A03

Shakespeare seems particularly interested in depicting heroic soldiers. Examples are: Macbeth, Othello, Hotspur (*Henry IV, Part 1*) and Mark Antony (*Antony and Cleopatra*). These soldiers are brave in battle but, tragically, bravery is no help to them in other kinds of situations. For example, Othello is unable to deal with his wife's perceived infidelity and Hotspur's scathing attack on Owen Glendower's magical powers breaks up the alliance against Henry IV.

ACT I SCENE 1

SUMMARY

- Three witches talk together during a thunderstorm.
- They plan to meet on the moorland again before sunset – knowing Macbeth will be there.
- Every detail of the first short scene evokes the supernatural.

ANALYSIS

MOOD AND ATMOSPHERE

The opening scene of the play is particularly important in establishing mood and atmosphere. The scene is set in an open and isolated place – the moorland is far removed from society and away from the usual social rules. The Witches themselves appear traditionally ugly, barely human. They can take the shape of animals, such as cats and toads. The weather too is poor and hostile to man: the 'fog and filthy air' (line 10) suggests darkness and unhealthiness. In this opening scene we are taken into a world of confusion. This is a place alien to human values, of darkness and foulness, and is a sinister challenge to ordinary goodness.

THE WITCHES' SPEECH

The Witches' use of rhyme is a feature of their speech. Used throughout the play, it brings to mind a sense of incantation and magical charms. In line 4, 'When the battles' lost and won', and line 9, 'Fair is foul and foul is fair', we are presented with a paradox. How can a battle be 'lost and won'? How can fair be foul? The phrases used seem to be impossible opposites and are only understandable to the Witches.

STUDY FOCUS: THE WITCHES IN CONTEXT — A04

The Witches would appear very real to a Jacobean audience. Witches were thought to be both political and spiritual traitors. In this opening scene they instantly create a sense of confusion, upsetting the natural order of things. This is echoed by the use of thunder and lightning, which was also associated with evil.

GLOSSARY

3	**Hurly burly**	turmoil, confusion
8	**Grey-Malkin**	grey cat
	Paddock	toad
	Anon	at once

CRITICAL VIEWPOINT A02

Right from the first scene *Macbeth* raises many questions, suggesting that ambiguity is at the heart of the play. We wonder how Macbeth will be involved in the Witches' evil. How does he fit into their plans? How is it possible that they know the outcome of the battle before it is over?

GRADE BOOSTER A02

If you are studying *Macbeth* for AQA/B, it is important to note that the **Gothic** element in this first scene is evident in the Witches' speech. The setting is also **Gothic** – a bleak and remote heath. The setting can be compared with the moors in *Wuthering Heights* and the Arctic (the starkest possible environment) in *Frankenstein*.

ACT I SCENE 2

SUMMARY

- King Duncan receives reports of battles being fought against his enemies.
- The reports stress the heroism of Macbeth and indicate his loyalty.
- Duncan condemns the Thane of Cawdor to death, for treachery.
- In gratitude, Duncan awards Macbeth the title of Thane of Cawdor.

ANALYSIS

ROYAL AUTHORITY

The military alarum (sound of trumpets) that begin this scene is in contrast to Scene 1, which opened with thunder and lightning and suggested evil. The play shifts from the wild world of the Witches to the place where the royal authority is demonstrated. The focus in this scene is on Macbeth and his virtues as a loyal soldier to King Duncan. The battle is given a size and an importance which magnify the qualities of Macbeth, and Duncan has nothing but praise for his heroic deeds. Our curiosity and anticipation are aroused and we want to meet this mighty champion. However, we recall the mention of his name by the Witches and this echo could cause us to question the authority and assurance displayed here.

A GOTHIC ELEMENT

Brutality and bloodshed is a theme in this scene, as shown by the very first words which are spoken by King Duncan – who fails to recognise his captain, 'What bloody man is that?' (line 1). Although the reports stress the heroism of Macbeth, they also stress his brutality, 'Till he unseame'd him from the nave to the chops' (line 22). That this brutality is seen as a virtue, 'O Valiant cousin! Worthy gentleman!' (line 24), gives the audience the impression that bloodshed is revelled in, creating a strongly **Gothic** element to the conflict here.

STUDY FOCUS: MACBETH'S CHARACTER — A03

Macbeth is seen in a positive light in these early scenes. We can look at other characters in other plays who are also seen in a good light early on, such as Antony in *Antony and Cleopatra* and the villain Iago in *Othello*. However, there are indications that Macbeth might have an element in his character that is not ideal. Although brave in battle, he is almost reckless. He is also brutal. These traits could be used for his destruction and might be seen as early character flaws.

GLOSSARY

13	**Kerns and galloglasses**	lightly armed soldiers and heavily armed soldiers
19	**valour's minion**	the favourite of bravery (meaning Macbeth)
22	**unseamed ... chops**	split Macdonwald from his navel to his jaws
25	**As ... reflection**	just as when the sun is bright too early (and the rest of the day is stormy and disappointing)
41	**memorise another Golgotha**	making the battle as famous for slaughter as Golgotha (place of the skulls), the site where Christ was crucified

CRITICAL VIEWPOINT — A02

The final line of this scene – 'what he hath lost, noble Macbeth hath won' (line 70) – reminds us of line 4 in Scene 1, and, it can be argued, it sets up an important connection between Macbeth and the Witches right from the start of the play. This connection is consolidated in Scene 3.

GRADE BOOSTER — A02

There is an important use of **dramatic irony** in this scene. Although Banquo is reported as being as valiant as Macbeth, he is overlooked by the king while Macbeth is honoured. The audience is aware that Macbeth is to become the next Thane of Cawdor but Macbeth himself, returning from the battlefield, is unaware of the honour. Think about the effect of this dramatic irony here.

CONTEXT A04

Among the writings of James VI of Scotland (who become James I of England) were works on poetry, kingship, the evils of tobacco and *Demonology* (1597), a study of witchcraft. James was the patron of Shakespeare's theatre company and *Macbeth* shows signs of having been written and performed for him.

ACT I SCENE 3

SUMMARY

- The Witches meet again, as planned, on a heath during a thunderstorm.
- They hail Macbeth as Thane of Glamis, Thane of Cawdor and future king.
- Banquo is told his descendants will be kings.
- The Witches vanish; Macbeth and Banquo debate as to what they are.
- Ross and Angus meet Macbeth and Banquo.
- Macbeth is shocked to hear that he is the new Thane of Cawdor.

ANALYSIS

THE WITCHES' POWERS

The scene opens with the Witches discussing the dreadful things they can do to men. However, there are limits to their powers. They can make the sea captain 'dwindle, peak, and pine' (line 23) but 'his bark cannot be lost' (line 24). As Macbeth and Banquo enter the heath, on their way home from their victorious battle, the Witches prepare themselves with a charm.

In the first two scenes, the world of the Witches has been separated from the world of men. The two worlds are now brought together. The Witches' conversation emphasises that although they cannot sink the sea-captain's boat, their evil and vindictive will cannot be thwarted by men, 'I'll drain him dry as hay' (line 18). Is this true? Their curse on the sea captain can be seen as a prediction of Macbeth's career.

THE WITCHES' IMPACT ON MACBETH AND BANQUO

GRADE BOOSTER A01

Look carefully at the language spoken between Macbeth and Banquo. Compare and contrast the way they both understand and react to the Witches' prophecies.

Macbeth's first line in the play 'so foul and fair a day I have not seen' (line 37) arrests us because it is so close to the Witches' speech at the end of Scene 1, 'Fair is foul and foul is fair' (1.11). It is as if Macbeth is already in tune with the Witches. The Witches ignore Banquo's questions and answer Macbeth. It is Macbeth they are interested in. He appears concerned and puzzled but Banquo is calm and sceptical. Macbeth commands the Witches to answer his questions 'Speak, I charge you!' (line 78) but the Witches fail to obey him. This is a key point when assessing to what extent Macbeth is master of his own destiny – and in fact argues against the idea that he has supernatural powers.

TRUTH OR LIES?

When Ross greets Macbeth as Thane of Cawdor, both Macbeth and Banquo are puzzled. Banquo is concerned that men are easily tempted into sin by 'instruments of darkness' (line 123). Macbeth's reaction is different; something within him seems to have been echoed in the Witches' words, and the prophecy appeals to his imagination. He ponders the possibility of becoming king, 'Two truths are told / As happy prologues to the swelling act / Of the imperial theme' (lines 126–8). The Witches' words raise the important question: is Macbeth's rise to becoming king inevitable or will he have to act?

STUDY FOCUS: THE WEIRD SISTERS `A02`

Shakespeare describes the Witches as 'the Weird sisters' but does not use the modern meaning of weird, which is 'peculiar'. The word comes from the Anglo-Saxon word for fate. Weird in this context means controlling human destiny and was spelled 'wyrd'. Whether or not Macbeth has the ability to shape his own destiny is a constant theme in the play, and the Witches are a symbol of this.

GLOSSARY

6	**Aroint thee**	get off
7	*Tiger*	there was an actual ship of this name which returned in 1606 after a bad voyage
8	**sieve**	witches defied the laws of nature
9	**rat ... tail**	witches took the shape of animals but not the tail
15–17	**ports ... card**	the witch controls all the winds and can cause them to blow from whichever unfavourable direction of the compass she chooses
20	**penthouse lid**	eyelid (like a sloping roof)
52	**fantastical**	imaginary
54	**present grace**	Thane of Glamis
55	**royal hope**	the throne of Scotland
70	**Sinell**	Macbeth's father
108	**borrowed robes**	the garments (and qualities) of another person
120	**enkindle**	encourage you to hope
155	**free hearts**	honest feelings

GRADE BOOSTER `A02`

If you are studying *Macbeth* for AQA/B, it is important to notice the two **Gothic** elements in this scene. As in Act I, the setting is on a bleak and remote heath. The **asides** spoken by Macbeth are also the beginning of a conspiracy, showing us another Gothic element in the play.

KEY QUOTATION: ACT I SCENE 3 `A01`

Key quotation: 'Come what come may, / Time and the hour runs through the roughest day' (lines 146–7)

- Macbeth is saying here that whatever is going to happen will happen, whatever the day looks like.
- Shakespeare's use of the rhyming couplet suggests that Macbeth does not want to think further on the matter of becoming king.
- We could argue, however, that Macbeth's very dismissal of the idea suggests its importance and that it will prey on his mind.

ACT I SCENE 4

SUMMARY

- In the palace at Forres, Malcolm, King Duncan's eldest son, reports the execution of the treacherous Cawdor to his father.
- Duncan greets Macbeth and Banquo warmly and announces that Malcolm is to be his heir.
- Macbeth ponders the fact that Malcolm is heir apparent and wonders how he will overcome that obstacle.
- Duncan has invited himself to be Macbeth's guest at Inverness.
- Macbeth sets off to inform his wife of the forthcoming royal visit.

ANALYSIS

CHECK THE FILM **A03**

In Roman Polanski's *Macbeth* (1971), the public execution of the Thane of Cawdor is a violent episode that is shown at length; in the play, we are simply told that it has been done.

ROYAL ORDER

In the palace at Forres, we are presented with a picture of royal order and justice. The description of the dying Cawdor as penitent and dignified is placed against the arrival of the new Thane of Cawdor – Macbeth. Malcolm's graciousness when speaking about Cawdor's death shows his nobility and gentility, 'Nothing in his life / Became him like the leaving it' (lines 8–9), and at the same time, Duncan shows himself to be an innocent and trusting person; speaking of the first Thane of Cawdor he states that 'He was a gentleman on whom I built / An absolute trust' (lines 14–15). There may be a hint that Duncan is not a good judge of character. Having noted how the first Thane of Cawdor proved to be a traitor, is he about to make the same mistake with Macbeth?

MACBETH'S RESPONSES

Macbeth answers Duncan's thanks using language that suggests obedience rather than warmth. There is an emphasis on 'service', 'loyalty', 'owe', 'your highness', 'duties', 'state', 'safe', 'love' and 'honour', all in half a dozen lines. Although Macbeth's words suggest a model of the loyal subject, his answers are not as warm as Banquo's responses. We already know another side to Macbeth. In contrast, Banquo thanks the king by merely completing the **metaphor** (of growing) used by Duncan – an appropriate and restrained reply.

NAMING A SUCCESSOR

Shakespeare's choice of this moment for Duncan to name a successor is very shrewd dramatically. Duncan's announcement forces into Macbeth's mind thoughts of the previous scene. He knows he cannot become king if Malcolm is to succeed Duncan, 'That is a step / On which I must fall down, or else o'erleap' (lines 49–50). The question is: why does Duncan name his successor at this point? In Scotland, at this time in history, a king's eldest son did not necessarily inherit the crown. By naming Malcolm, Duncan runs the risk of disappointing other potential candidates, including his nephew Macbeth. We could therefore see this action as an error of judgement on Duncan's behalf.

STUDY FOCUS: DISGUISE | A04

To get the best grades at AS and A2, you will need to be aware of the context behind the lines spoken in a play. Take lines 12 to 13: 'There's no art / To find the mind's construction in the face'. This describes the possible disparity between a person's pleasing appearance and the reality of their wicked nature. The theme of a person's true nature and how they appear is a constant presence in Shakespeare's drama. See, for example, how the villain Iago appears to Othello. The very business of acting in the theatre presents a truth to us – that humans are capable of disguising themselves. People can pretend to be something they are not. Look out for this in Act I Scene 6.

KEY QUOTATION: ACT I SCENE 4 | A01

Key quotation: 'We will establish our estate upon / Our eldest, Malcolm, whom we name hereafter / The Prince of Cumberland' (lines 38–40).

- Duncan is saying that he will leave his kingdom to his eldest son, Malcolm, who will now be given the title of Prince of Cumberland.

- Duncan may be thinking that he is securing his kingdom by naming Malcolm as his successor.

- Duncan could have named Macbeth as successor, so this may indicate that he believes Malcolm has greater kingly qualities than Macbeth.

GRADE BOOSTER | A01

Malcolm is very positive about how the Thane of Cawdor conducted himself before he died. What does this tell us about Cawdor and what does this tell us about Malcolm?

GLOSSARY

2	**in commission**	authorised to conduct the execution
3	**liege**	lord
10	**that ... studied**	who had learned a part (like an actor)
12–13	**There's no art ... face**	there is no certain way of knowing a man's character from his face
46	**harbinger**	messenger (originally an official sent ahead to arrange accommodation for the king)
59	**kinsman**	Macbeth is Duncan's first cousin

ACT I SCENE 5

SUMMARY

- Lady Macbeth reads a letter from her husband.
- She immediately looks forward to the fulfilment of the Witches' prophecy but believes Macbeth is too mild to seize the throne.
- A servant brings news of the king's impending arrival.
- Macbeth arrives at the castle.

CHECK THE BOOK A03

The castle, as a setting for murder, can be compared with *The Bloody Chamber* where the Marquis has murdered and hidden his wives. It is worth remembering that a castle, a conspiracy and horrific secrets are common features of **Gothic** literature.

ANALYSIS

LADY MACBETH'S RUTHLESSNESS

There is no audience preparation for the character of Macbeth's wife. She appears in this scene as a ruthless woman who is committed to strive for the greater glory of her husband. If he is king, she will be queen. Macbeth's ability to speculate and think around problems (see Act I Scene 3) is seen by Lady Macbeth as a crucial weakness. She believes her husband does not lack ambition but she perceives that he is squeamish about the method to achieve this ambition. The steely determination required to commit an assassination must come from her.

LADY MACBETH AND THE WITCHES

There is an element in Lady Macbeth's attitude strongly reminiscent of the Witches. She talks of pouring her spirits in Macbeth's ear as if it is some potion to alter his character. She also asks evil spirits to defeminise her and to dehumanise her by entering her body, 'Come, you spirits … fill me from crown to the toe top-full / Of direst cruelty' (lines 38–40). It appears that they oblige – for a time. Just like Macbeth in the previous scene, she prays for darkness to hide her planned action, 'Come thick night / And pall thee in the dunnest smoke of hell' (lines 48–9). It is no wonder that some critics see her as the fourth witch. The chain of imperatives ('come', 'fill', etc) gives her speech a special urgency and determination. She is aware of Macbeth's impending arrival and has more or less completed her cry for evil to fill her when Macbeth enters.

THE MARITAL RELATIONSHIP

When Macbeth appears, there is little trace of endearment from his wife. He has just returned from battle and has put his life at risk. Lady Macbeth appears not to acknowledge or to appreciate that he has returned safely and instead immediately forces Macbeth to see himself in terms of her plan for power. She addresses him as he had been addressed by the Witches in Scene 3, 'Great Glamis, worthy Cawdor' (line 52) and 'Greater than both by the all-hail hereafter' (line 53). The arrival of the messenger announcing Duncan's visit is a brilliant dramatic stroke. The audience is aware that Duncan is coming, what is so startling is the messenger's arrival immediately after Lady Macbeth has voiced her plans: 'The King comes here tonight' (line 28) is the anticipation of her dearest wish. We are left wondering why Shakespeare presents Lady Macbeth as the stronger partner in the marriage at this point in the play. While Macbeth pondered and wondered if 'chance will have me king,' (I.3.143), Lady Macbeth is actively planning the murder.

STUDY FOCUS: THE IDEA OF CHARACTER A03

Shakespeare thought of character in a different way from how we see it today. Although his characters show great depth of feeling, they were often drawn from prototypes and audiences would have expected them to behave in certain ways. He was interested in themes and, at times, character took second place. After the emergence of psychology during the late 1800s onwards, the idea of 'character' changed to become more about the individual, and Sigmund Freud (1856–1939) found much that fascinated him in Shakespeare's plays. He discussed the relationship between Macbeth and Lady Macbeth in *Some Character Types Met With in Psycho-Analytical Work* (1916). He wrote that 'what he [Macbeth] feared in his pangs of conscience is fulfilled in her; she becomes all remorse and he defiance. Together they exhaust the possibilities of reaction to the crime, like two disunited parts of a single psychical individuality, and it may be that they are both copied from the same prototype.' It is worth reflecting on Freud's views as you study the play.

BANQUO'S WARNING

In Act 1 Scene 3, Banquo cautions Macbeth that the Witches can 'Win us with honest trifles, to betray's / In deepest consequence' (lines 124–5). He could be warning Macbeth that the Witches are temptresses who are telling him some truths to incite him to commit a great evil, the consequences of which will far outweigh the benefits they are offering. Banquo notices that Macbeth was impressed by the Witches' prophecies and suspects that he will prove to be disloyal to the king. However, Banquo is also impressed by the Witches when it comes to the prophecy about his sons becoming kings, perhaps suggesting that he too is susceptible to the lure of power.

GLOSSARY

2	**perfectest report**	the best knowledge (either Macbeth has made enquiries about the Witches or his own experience has proved them right)
26	**golden round**	crown
27	**metaphysical**	supernatural
36	**raven**	bird announcing death

REVISION FOCUS: TASK 1 A02

How far do you agree with the statements below?

- The mortals in *Macbeth* are more evil than the witches.
- The reintroduction of Banquo just before Macbeth kills King Duncan is important for the development of plot and character.

Try writing opening paragraphs for essays based on the discussion points above.

CONTEXT A04

A black cloth was hung on the stage during tragedies; the roof of the stage was called the 'heavens'. The 'pall' and 'heaven' of Lady Macbeth's curse may refer to these (lines 49 and 51). Shakespeare's plays often contain allusions like this to the situation and techniques of dramatic performance.

ACT I SCENE 6

SUMMARY

- Duncan arrives at Macbeth's castle. He notices the pleasant air.
- Duncan and his nobles are welcomed by Lady Macbeth.
- He is full of compliments towards Lady Macbeth and she returns them.

ANALYSIS

PEACE AND TREACHERY

Duncan and Banquo admire the peaceful location and atmosphere at Macbeth's castle. This is highly ironic, as we know Macbeth and Lady Macbeth plan to kill Duncan inside the castle. Lady Macbeth welcomes Duncan and they exchange greetings and compliments. This 'pleasant exchange' further alienates Lady Macbeth from the audience. The emphasis of this scene, as in Scene 4, is on peace, trust and courtesy – all of which are about to be destroyed. After the passion and vicious emotions of Scene 5, we are presented with images of tranquillity. The words 'guest' and 'host' are repeated. Lady Macbeth appears as the perfect, sophisticated hostess but we remember her advice to her husband: 'look like the innocent flower, / But be the serpent under't (I.5. 63–4). She is acting out the advice she gave her husband to perfection.

STUDY FOCUS: THE DIVINE RIGHT OF KINGS — A04

It was a commonly held belief that kings were placed on the throne by God. The 'divine right of kings' is a belief asserting that a monarch is subject to no earthly authority, deriving his right to rule directly from the will of God. The doctrine implies that any attempt to depose or murder the king runs contrary to the will of God and is a sacrilegious act. The theory of divine right justified the king's absolute authority in both political and spiritual matters and was a strongly held belief in England under the reign of James I who wrote books about it from 1597 to 1598.

GLOSSARY

7	**coign of vantage**	suitable corner
20	**We rest your hermits**	we still pray for you
25–8	**Your servants … your own**	Lady Macbeth means all that belongs to Macbeth really belongs to the king, and he can claim any of it at any time
31	**By your leave**	with your permission (he would kiss Lady Macbeth on the cheek)

CHECK THE FILM A03

This scene, which conjures up an agreeable picture of Macbeth's home, is left out of Roman Polanski's *Macbeth* (1971). Duncan's misguided confidence in the hospitality that awaits him is lost in the film, therefore. However, a moment of calm, such as this scene, is at odds with Polanski's relentlessly grim and mud-bespattered version of medieval life.

CRITICAL VIEWPOINT A03

James I was the patron of Shakespeare's company, so we could argue that Shakespeare portrays Duncan's murder as an act against God in order to please his king and patron.

CONTEXT A04

Banquo speaks of the 'temple-haunting martlet' (line 4), which is the house martin. House martins like to nest in the eaves of tall buildings, such as churches and castles. It is said that the house martin nests in a place where love is present. This is ironic, as the hosts are not about to demonstrate love for their king.

ACT I SCENE 7

SUMMARY

- Macbeth reflects on the crime he is about to commit.
- He decides not to kill Duncan as he fears the consequences but Lady Macbeth persuades him to go through with it.
- She outlines her tactics and Macbeth admires her resolution.
- Macbeth steels himself for the regicide.

ANALYSIS

MACBETH'S INNER DEBATE

Macbeth's final words in Scene 5 were: 'We will speak further' (line 69). His wavering is continued into the present scene. He fears life after death and his very real concerns are that, if he murders Duncan, who 'Hath borne his faculties so meek' (line 16), then he, Macbeth, will face an eternity of divine punishment. He continues his reflection later on in his **soliloquy** when he expresses the fear that Duncan's virtues 'Will plead like angels' (line 19). Macbeth is also concerned that if he murders the king, when he becomes king others may do the same and he will be murdered in turn: 'that we but teach / Bloody instructions, which, being taught, return / To plague the inventor' (lines 8–10). He also recognises that as host he should 'shut the door' (line 15) and protect his guest. He is aware that 'vaulting ambition' (line 27) is his only reason for killing Duncan, which he realises is an untrustworthy motive.

MACBETH'S MASCULINITY

When Lady Macbeth joins her husband, they do not conduct a real discussion – she tells Macbeth what has to be done. Macbeth has allowed himself to imagine the future beyond the murder, but Lady Macbeth refuses to think beyond the present. We could argue that Macbeth's will is weakened by speculation but her will is strengthened by concentrating solely on the act of killing Duncan. It is the difference between 'why?' and 'how?' Lady Macbeth's main argument is that her husband has to prove his manhood by acting decisively. He knows there is another concept of manhood (lines 46–7), one perhaps based on honour and duty: 'all that may become a man' (line 46). However, he is dominated by a woman prepared to renounce the essence of her femininity. Eventually, his argument is reduced to the cowardly 'If we should fail?' (line 59). Failure is not something that Lady Macbeth wishes to contemplate.

STUDY FOCUS: MACBETH'S FINAL TWO SPEECHES [A02]

In Macbeth's final two speeches in this scene, he adopts the manner of speaking of his wife. He echoes Lady Macbeth's earlier sentiments (see I.5.61–4) in his last couplet – which is not accidental. We are left wondering if he admires his wife or if he is reduced to sarcasm. We do know that the preparations for the murder are complete – and await the next scene.

STUDY FOCUS: THE PERSUASIVE TECHNIQUES OF A DOMINANT WIFE

A02

For a modern audience, it is difficult to imagine the shocking, even comic, impact of seeing Macbeth so easily overruled by his wife. In Shakespeare's time it would have been taken for granted that a man is superior to a woman in mind, will and body. However, if we look at the language she uses, she accuses him of allowing fear to get the better of his desire to kill Duncan. She uses a **simile** 'Like the poor cat in the adage' (line 45) to back up her argument – meaning that Macbeth is like a cat that wants a fish but refuses to wet its paws. She then accuses her husband of being a beast by suggesting the plan to kill Duncan in the first place. Looking back at Scene 5, Macbeth does not suggest the murder of Duncan, even though he has privately considered regicide. Her persuasive techniques continue when she accuses Macbeth of acting in a cowardly way and says that, although a woman, she would have the courage to kill the king had she 'so sworn as you' (line 58). With these words, she tries to goad him into action.

CONTEXT

A04

From the perspective of the twenty-first century, it is easy to forget that, until quite recently, society upheld a Christian worldview. Macbeth's concerns about divine punishment due to the murder of a king would be very real to his audience.

GLOSSARY

s.d	***Sewer***	the equivalent of a modern head waiter (originally the person who tested the food given to the king)
	divers	various
3	**trammel**	catch together, like a net
4	**with his surcease success**	what I want (success) by his death
10	**even-handed**	impartial
17	**faculties**	powers (as king)
20	**taking-off**	departure, murder
22	**striding the blast**	astride the storm (of protest)
45	**adage**	proverb

ACT II SCENE 1

SUMMARY

- After midnight, Banquo and his son, Fleance, meet Macbeth in the castle courtyard.
- Banquo passes on Duncan's compliments to Macbeth together with the gift of a diamond for Lady Macbeth.
- Macbeth advises Banquo to side with him in the future and Banquo makes it clear to Macbeth that he will only act honourably.
- Macbeth awaits the signal to kill Duncan.

ANALYSIS

A SENSE OF FOREBODING

Banquo's uneasiness together with his speech about his 'cursèd thoughts when sleeping' (line 8) gives us a sense of restless anxiety. Shakespeare often uses foreboding in his plays – it heightens our feeling of suspense and draws us into the action of the plot. When Macbeth suddenly appears from the darkness, the two converse politely although both are aware of the Witches' predictions. The present of the diamond for Lady Macbeth also contributes to the mood of apprehension. A diamond was regarded as a charm against witchcraft and nightmares, so does his gift to Lady Macbeth leave Duncan unprotected?

BANQUO, MACBETH AND WITCHCRAFT

Banquo and Macbeth meet immediately before the murder and it would seem, from lines 7–9 and line 20, that the meeting with the Witches has made a lasting impression on Banquo's mind. He is deeply disturbed by the workings of his subconscious in dreams. Ultimately, Banquo's trust rests on God's 'merciful powers' (line 7). In contrast, Macbeth has an imaginative flight in this scene and allies himself with witchcraft, murder and secrecy, 'witchcraft celebrates … withered Murder' (lines 51–2). He associates the forthcoming murder of Duncan with 'Tarquin's ravishing strides' (line 55). Tarquin (son of the King of Rome) raped his hostess at night. It would seem that Macbeth is influenced by the Witches but Banquo relies on God and is able to put his nightmares behind him.

STUDY FOCUS: THE DAGGER • A01

During his **soliloquy** Macbeth asks the question, 'Is this a dagger which I see before me' (line 33). He feels that it might be a 'dagger of the mind' (line 38). He also sees the dagger as 'in form as palpable / As this which now I draw' (lines 40–1). Shakespeare keeps the two possibilities open to us: 1) the dagger is a dagger of Macbeth's imagination; 2) the dagger is conjured by the Witches to spur Macbeth on to kill Duncan. These two possibilities maintain the ambiguity surrounding the supernatural forces in the play.

CRITICAL VIEWPOINT • A03

'The role of the Witches in *Macbeth* is to warn of the dangers of the supernatural.' Try considering the role of the Witches in *Macbeth* in the light of this suggestion.

GLOSSARY

14	**largess**	generous gifts
28	**bosom … clear**	heart free from guilt and loyalty unspoiled
40	**palpable**	real, able to be touched
46	**dudgeon**	handle
63	**knell**	bell sounded to announce a death

EXTENDED COMMENTARY

ACT II SCENE 1 LINES 31–64

This **soliloquy** comes after the supper guests have retired to bed and immediately before the murder of Duncan. In Act I Scene 7 we heard Macbeth wrestling with his conscience and finally being forced into preparedness by the forcefulness of his wife. Immediately after the murder Macbeth is almost helpless with anxiety and cannot pull his mind away from his experience in Duncan's bedroom. By Act II Scene 3 he has partially recovered, although his speech in lines 88–93 seems to hark back to Act I Scene 7.

This placing of the soliloquy may seem over-elaborate but no scene in a play operates independently of others around it, and our awareness of this context gives added richness to the particular passage. For example, at the end of Act I Scene 7 Macbeth's words echo the resolution of his wife's earlier words:

> I am settled; and bend up
> Each corporal agent to this terrible feat.
> Away, and mock the time with fairest show:
> False face must hide what the false heart doth know. (I.7.79–82)

Yet, left on his own, Macbeth's mind conjures up hallucinations and he is fearful and afraid – he is shown to be the opposite of the 'settled' man that he claims to be. This is further highlighted in the following scene when his self-control has collapsed and he is tormented by the noises around him: 'How is't with me when every noise appals me?' (II.2.58).

Although the content of the soliloquy reveals Macbeth's uncertainty and doubt, the regular verse creates a contrasting sense of stability. There is only one interruption (the bell) and there is only one character present – Macbeth. The fact that the thoughts of Macbeth are presented as a soliloquy is important because it means that what we are hearing is heard by no other character in the play and Macbeth can speak his mind frankly – he has nobody to deceive but himself.

The soliloquy is Macbeth's final preparation of himself before the murder. What might we expect him to think about? The plan? The fear of discovery? What he must do as soon as the murder is committed? None of these things is directly addressed by Macbeth; in fact, rather than wondering about the difficulty of the task, he uses his imagination to shift his mind from the events before him. His imagined dagger appears to have a will of its own, 'Thou marshall'st me' (line 42), yet Macbeth pushes the dagger from his mind and replaces it with an atmosphere suitable to his intention and he thinks of the figures of murder – the wolf and Tarquin.

If we look in detail at the soliloquy we see that there are four parts to it: 1) lines 33–49, concerning the dagger; 2) lines 49–56, voicing Macbeth's reverie on the world outside; 3) lines 56–60, an invocation to the earth; and 4) lines 60–4, he moves into action. How does Macbeth's mind move from one unit to the next? The dagger suddenly arrives in the air and in line 48 Macbeth exerts his reason and he attributes the appearance of the dagger to his preoccupation with the murder plan. The second part is the result of Macbeth

GRADE BOOSTER **A02**

It is interesting to see how Macbeth operates at this stage. Only when his mind is fully prepared, is he ready to act .

looking away from the dagger but his thoughts remain obstinately on the idea of the murder. The word 'Nature' should be a contrary force to his hallucination but to Macbeth it 'seems dead' and allows 'wicked dreams' to deceive sleeping man (line 50), indicating that he is still hallucinating. The ghost-like movement of Murder stalking his victim leads into the insistence on quietness in the third part. The final part is a break from the preceding lines. Here Macbeth repeats instructions to himself as if still unsure of what he is doing. Notice also that the threats he refers to have not taken place as yet – but he has filled in the time while awaiting the signal without losing his nerve. It is significant that Macbeth does not mention any person around him – not even his wife. It is also significant that he avoids naming his victim until the second last line!

This is not a heavily **metaphorical** passage like some that occur elsewhere in the play but there are some interesting choices of language. There is a move from sights to sounds in the soliloquy matching the furtiveness and tension of Macbeth. Human beings (but Macbeth really means himself) are represented as being strangely passive in a world where objects and abstract ideas take control: the dagger offers its handle and indicates directions; the eyes are made fools of; the 'bloody business' 'informs' and dreams 'abuse'; the bell 'invites' or 'summons'. Of course, the dagger itself with its suggestive movements and drops of blood is an image of Macbeth's troubled conscience which he cannot control ('clutch') or be sure about. The 'heat-oppressèd brain' which creates the elusive dagger is the same brain that is needed for the 'heat of deeds'. In the **imagery** of witchcraft and murder the concentration is on the sacrifice of innocence (the 'curtained sleep' and the pure Lucretia) by a secret and ruthless power. The only colours present in the soliloquy are those of darkness and blood.

The structure and syntax of the soliloquy reveals further tension in Macbeth's mind. The opening lines are marked by questions, exclamations, qualifications and repetitions, all suggesting uncertainty and anxiety. In the middle parts, longer sentences with lots of adjectives create a sense of deliberation and suspense as well as intensity. The final part seems to offer resolution to the questions and doubts raised at the beginning of the passage. However, this resolution is so repetitive and so tidily arranged that we suspect something glib and mechanical in it – it seems that Macbeth has not set his mind at rest.

GRADE BOOSTER A02

By focusing on particular dramatic conventions – soliloquy, dialogue and so on – you can explore their function. In this case, Macbeth's soliloquy reveals the true state of his mind. He ponders if the daggers are from his feverish mind. He mentions nightmares and wolves – he recalls the story of Tarquin and relates that story to his own situation.

ACT II SCENE 2

SUMMARY

- Lady Macbeth has drugged the guards and become 'bold' through drinking wine.
- Macbeth enters the scene, having killed Duncan.
- Lady Macbeth takes charge of the situation.
- There is a knocking at the gate.
- Macbeth reveals that he regrets killing Duncan.

ANALYSIS

SUSPENSE

This is a scene of intense excitement. The suspense is heightened by Lady Macbeth's vivid recounting of her preparations. It is also heightened by her jumpiness. She does not know the outcome – Macbeth might have failed to carry out the regicide or he might have been caught. This suspense is not relieved by the return of Macbeth with the news 'I have done the deed' (line 14). Macbeth's state of mind verges on the hysterical and his extreme tension is communicated to us. We are forced to participate in it by the abrupt changes of direction in the speech of the characters. There are interruptions, sudden noises, questions and exclamations.

MACBETH'S ANGUISH

Shakespeare intends us to be trapped in Macbeth's anguish but also allows us to identify with Lady Macbeth, as she struggles for control. We see the bloody daggers in Macbeth's hands and identify with both characters as they fear discovery. We are involved and feel a complicity in the murder, understanding that Macbeth cannot go back with the daggers and that the risk of discovery is great. The tension is abruptly punctured by the knocking at the door, like the police arriving at the scene of the crime. Macbeth's hysteria is only calmed by the masterful Lady Macbeth. However,  the scene ends with Macbeth's regret, 'Wake Duncan with thy knocking! I would thou couldst' (line 74), as he recognises the enormity of his crime. We feel, at this point, that he does not care if he is discovered or not.

LADY MACBETH'S REACTION

In this scene, Lady Macbeth is by far the stronger of the two. Although Macbeth has proved himself to be a brave soldier, he is shocked by the cold-blooded murder he has committed. Lady Macbeth chides Macbeth that although her hands are of the same colour (red) she would 'shame / To wear a heart so white' (line 65). She believes that 'A little water clears us of this deed' (line 67), suggesting that the crime could simply be washed away and their consciences cleansed. At this point she makes no allowance for the guilt Macbeth feels and has not considered how their relationship may suffer. Her reaction is very different to that of her husband – who is already full of regrets. We remember that she has invited evil spirits into her body and she has renounced her femininity, and this fits with the lack of compassion and humanity she shows.

CHECK THE BOOK **A03**

For a comparably evil protagonist in a very different type of play, read or watch Shakespeare's *Richard III*. This is a tragedy in which we are hardly made to sympathise in any way with the protagonist. We might possibly admire his evil gusto but may feel he deserves his downfall and death. Another interesting Shakespearean portrayal of human wickedness is Edmund in *King Lear*. Like Macbeth, his wickedness is fuelled by jealousy of others.

STUDY FOCUS: SLEEP AND PRAYER   A04

To kill Duncan, Macbeth had to walk past the king's sons. They are praying as they sleep and Macbeth is concerned that he cannot say amen to their prayers. The inability to say a prayer, or to say amen, was thought to be a sign of being bewitched. Macbeth also believes he will never sleep soundly again. Perhaps he is afraid to sleep because of the possibility of nightmares? Or perhaps his conscience will not allow him to sleep? Sleep is seen as something for the innocent here and Macbeth is no longer innocent. He murdered Duncan whilst Duncan slept and now feels that he 'shall sleep no more' (line 43). This short phrase creates a perfect circle of cause and effect, as Macbeth's crime is translated into his punishment.

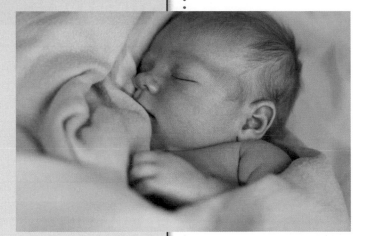

The list of metaphorical descriptions of sleep (lines 36–40) is an example of poetical **rhetorical figurative** writing, inventing fanciful **epithets** for a single subject. Is Macbeth reciting something he has already learned by heart, or does this poetic list suggest the seething imagination of his sleepless, hallucinatory state? The hectic pace of the play suggests he has not slept since the battle with which the play begins, and his speech is an echo of this fact.

GLOSSARY

5	**surfeited grooms**	drunken servants
6	**charge**	duty
	possets	bedtime drinks
39	**second course**	the most nourishing course of a meal
52	**infirm**	weak
62	**multitudinous**	extensive
	incarnadine	turn red

CONTEXT   A04

Magic powers and their usage was a subject that fascinated many of Shakespeare's contemporaries. One of the best-known figures of the age was Dr John Dee (1527–1608). As well as being an excellent mathematician, Dee also studied astrology and sorcery. It is possible that he believed his studies of the occult would allow him to call up spirits and control their actions. Dee's library was torched in the hope that this would put an end to his unnatural studies.

ACT II SCENE 3

SUMMARY

- A drunken porter comes to open the gates.
- He is annoyed that he has been disturbed and pretends to be the porter of hell.
- Macduff, the Thane of Fife, discovers the king is dead.
- Lady Macbeth faints.
- Malcolm and Donalbain, fearing for their lives, decide to flee.
- Lennox talks of the disturbed night.

ANALYSIS

THE PORTER'S SPEECH

The tension of the previous scene is maintained by the knocking at the gate. It is further heightened by our feeling that the discovery of the murder is merely being delayed by the rambling talk and the horror of the murder is intensified by the coarse vulgarity of the Porter. It seems, in his comic bad taste, to be a gruesome attempt to cover up the truth – although the Porter knows nothing of the murder. We, however, are kept in suspense.

When we examine the words more carefully, the Porter gives a contemporary and universal significance to Macbeth's crimes. He pretends to be the porter of hell, admitting imaginary sinners. This links back to Act I, Scene 7 – when Macbeth was concerned about his eternal destiny.

Some film and theatre producers have made the Porter scene comic in terms of his actions and speech. They have interpreted this scene as a relief from the high drama of the murder. Certainly some of the porter's comments would have made the Jacobean audience laugh. For example, 'Faith here's an English tailor come hither, for stealing out of a French hose' (line 8) suggests that the English tailor bought French hose (cloth) which was wide and full. The English tailor reshaped it to make the hose into a tight garment and used the extra cloth to make another garment – thus making a dishonest profit. The reference to clothing reminds us of Banquo's comment in Act I Scene 4 about Macbeth's unfitness to rule.

> **GRADE BOOSTER** **A02**
>
> Consider the careful and deliberate way in which Shakespeare introduces Macduff into the narrative. He is added at this point so that he cannot be implicated in the regicide. We may wonder where he was during the battle. He finds the murdered king and there is a sense of shock at the discovery.

CHAOS AND CONFUSION

Macbeth and Lady Macbeth's actions and words are a mixture of the extravagant and plausible. It is interesting to compare Macbeth's words in lines 88–93 with his speech in Act V Scene 5 lines 17–28. In lines 88–93, Macbeth pretends that, with the death of Duncan, the best of life is gone, but by Act V Scene 5 lines 17–28, he knows the best has gone. Banquo, more than Macbeth, proves himself to be the master of the situation and his speech near the end of the scene is judicious, firm and clear spoken. The flight of Malcolm and Donalbain is an intimation of the distrust and moral confusion that is soon to be seen as characteristic of Macbeth's behaviour as king.

MACBETH'S MORAL DECLINE

In this scene we witness the further moral decline of Macbeth. At the start of the play, he was a respected soldier, newly honoured by Duncan and described by the king as a 'peerless kinsman' (I.4.59). Now knowing the king is dead, Macbeth is forced to lie to Macduff and Lennox. Macbeth has also murdered the sleeping guards to conceal his actions and tells Lennox 'I do repent me of my fury / That I did kill them' (II.3.104–5). He makes excuses for murdering the guards and, at this point, Lady Macbeth faints. Has she fainted to distract the questioners or is she suddenly overcome with the enormity of her crime? It would appear that Macbeth has now collected himself sufficiently to be able to cover his tracks by killing the guards, covering the evidence, and telling untruths.

STUDY FOCUS: THE UNRULY NIGHT — A04

Lennox mentions that the 'night has been unruly'(line 51). The lamentations (wailings) heard suggest that all of nature is in turmoil due to the king's murder. We are reminded that the Jacobeans believed in a divine order. This order was decided by God, who they believed was ultimately in control of the universe. A crime against the king, therefore, was a crime against God. This belief was linked to Satan's rebellion against God in the Bible. Satan was deemed responsible for unrest and it was believed that he worked through witches and evil spirits to attack the divine order that God had installed. In this speech, we are made aware that Macbeth is now on the side of evil. Shakespeare gives us a glimpse of what is to happen during Macbeth's reign as king. There will be 'dire combustion' (terrible civil unrest) and this idea is explored further in Act II Scene 4.

GLOSSARY

4	**Belzebub**	Satan
8	**equivocater**	one who tampers with the truth to suit his argument
18	**primrose … bonfire**	the seductive, pleasurable way to hell
69	**Gorgon**	anyone who looked at this mythical monster was turned to stone
108	**pauser**	what should make one hesitate
123	**naked frailties**	underclad bodies (but this also implies human vulnerability)

CHECK THE BOOK — A03

Read De Quincey's famous short essay 'On the Knocking at the Gate in *Macbeth*' (first published in the London Magazine, 1823) for a brilliant if eccentric account of the effects of this moment in the play.

GRADE BOOSTER — A02

We understand how much Macbeth is equivocating in the speeches that express shock at Duncan's murder. Can we detect his dishonesty from his mode of speech?

ACT II SCENE 4

SUMMARY

- Ross discusses omens with an old man.
- Macduff reports that suspicion falls upon Malcolm and Donalbain.
- Macbeth has gone to Scone to be crowned king.
- Macduff refuses to attend the coronation.

CONTEXT **A04**

The play *Macbeth* was probably first performed indoors at court and at night rather than in the daylight of an open-air theatre such as the Globe. The constant references to night-time reinforce this likelihood.

ANALYSIS

AN OUTSIDER'S VIEW

In this scene we receive a view of the incident from people not directly involved in it. The Old Man, significantly given the biblical span of life (seventy years) is used by Shakespeare to represent the common man and his point of view. The murder of Duncan is unique in the Old Man's experience and we could argue that this makes it even more horrific.

AN UNNATURAL NIGHT

The idea that human wickedness is reflected by turmoil in the natural world is common to other Shakespearian tragedies. The storm in *King Lear* is an obvious example. Here, although it is now day, night is still predominant. It is as if night is shielding us from the murder.

Unnatural events occur – such as a 'mousing owl', which is usually seen flying close to the ground, killing a high-flying falcon. Duncan's horses become uncontrollable and, apparently, eat each other. Shakespeare allows his audience to see that when God's appointed representative is murdered, the whole of nature is disturbed. James I was fearful of an assassination – there were several attempts against his life – so it is likely that he would have approved of this scene. The consequences of killing a king are portrayed as so terrible that the attempt would not be worth contemplating. Although the events Shakespeare describes in this scene appear somewhat fanciful to us, the Jacobeans would have seen them as quite plausible, such was their belief in divine order and its reflection in the whole of nature.

THE FINGER OF SUSPICION

This scene advances the plot in providing two pieces of key information. Macduff confirms that the guards are believed to be responsible for Duncan's death – and it is revealed that Macduff will not attend Macbeth's coronation at Scone. Ross asks what they hoped to gain from Duncan's murder, the assumption being that Malcolm and Donalbain must have arranged the murder of their father because they fled the scene of the crime.

There is a hint that Macduff is suspicious of Macbeth when he informs Ross that he may '**see things well done there**' (line 37), that is, at Scone. This could suggest that Macduff believes Macbeth will become a tyrant in the future. There is a warning for the future too as Macduff comments that '**our old robes sit easier than our new**' (line 38). We find ourselves asking the question, does Macduff think that Macbeth might be implicated in the murder?

STUDY FOCUS: ROSS IN CONTEXT — A03

Ross intends to travel to Scone, where Scottish kings were crowned. Some commentators have argued that Ross is a person who looks after his own interests. Despite the fact that Macduff is not going to the coronation but travelling back to his castle at Fife, Ross still intends to show his loyalty – which would please Macbeth. The scene appears to end with a human and Christian hope that traditional values will be restored. Knowing the different reactions of Macduff and Ross, what do the Old Man's last lines indicate? Could he be blessing those who wish to put bad to right or is he gently chiding Ross for seeing good in evil deeds?

CRITICAL VIEWPOINT — A02

The significance of the dialogue between the Old Man and Ross is that they add to the description given by Lennox in the previous scene (lines 52–9). This shows us the importance Shakespeare gives to the disruption of nature after the murder of Duncan.

KEY QUOTATION: ACT II SCENE 4 — A01

Key quotation: 'Thriftless ambition, that will raven up / Thine own life's means' (II.4.28–9).

- Ross is saying it is a stupid ambition that causes a son to kill the father who supports him.
- Ross is talking about the king's sons' supposed involvement with the murder of Duncan.
- Ross is implying that Macbeth might not be innocent.

GLOSSARY

7	**travelling lamp**	sun
13	**mousing**	(usually content to) hunt mice
15	**minions**	darlings, best
24	**suborned**	paid to commit a crime
28	**Thriftless**	wasteful
	raven up	ravenously devour
32	**invested**	crowned as king
40	**benison**	blessing
41	**good ... foes**	see the best in people (a reference to the peacemakers of the Bible)

ACT III SCENE 1

SUMMARY

- Banquo remembers the Witches' prophecies and suspects Macbeth of Duncan's murder.
- Macbeth has settled into the royal palace at Forres.
- He is jealous of Banquo's good qualities.
- He arranges for the murder of Banquo and his son, Fleance.

ANALYSIS

MACBETH'S AND BANQUO'S THOUGHTS

We see Macbeth, in this scene, as the established king but his mind is not secure. Shakespeare arranges the thoughts of Banquo and Macbeth in parallel so that they refer forward and back to each other. This means that we hear Banquo's thoughts of Macbeth before we hear any of the king's own. Banquo says nothing of Macbeth's qualities as a king or even as a man, whereas Macbeth presents a generous analysis of Banquo's character. Both men seem to be obsessed by the predictions of the Witches concerning the descendants of Banquo. Macbeth, however, thinks that he can negate the prediction by killing Banquo and Fleance – even though the prophecies have been proved correct in his own case.

STUDY FOCUS: MACBETH AS A SCHEMER — A01

Notice the casual skill with which Macbeth ascertains Banquo's movements. He takes care to avoid any suspicion and to mention repeatedly the importance he places on Banquo's presence at the special supper in the evening and at the meeting the following day. It seems curious that Shakespeare devotes so much time (about seventy lines) to Macbeth's meeting with the two Murderers. The organisation and manipulation of other people are marks of a tyrant. 'To be thus is nothing; / But to be safely thus!' (lines 47–8) he says while waiting for them. Perhaps his elaborate briefing is an attempt to persuade himself of how foolproof his plan is. He, paradoxically, appeals to them as men – yet murdering unsuspecting victims is not a manly attribute.

MACBETH'S MOTIVATION

Macbeth wants Banquo killed for more than one reason. He believes his 'genius is rebuked' by Banquo and Banquo has already refused to join him in any duplicity (see II.1.26–9). Macbeth also knows that Banquo 'chid the sisters / When first they put the name of king upon him' (lines 56–7). Banquo, at that point, saw the Witches for what they were – evil spirits. Remembering the Witches' prophecy that Banquo's children will become kings, Macbeth is also fearful that he has committed his terrible acts only so that Banquo and his descendants will benefit. He now seeks to defy fate by murdering Banquo and his young son, Fleance, despite the fact that nothing so far has prevented the Witches' prophecies coming true for himself.

CRITICAL VIEWPOINT A03

A psychological reading of the play would explore Macbeth's motives in hiring murderers. Is it that it is simply too difficult to commit the act now that he is king? Or is he unable to face the physical reality of murder?

THE WITCHES' PROPHECIES

The Witches' predictions recur throughout the play as if they (the Witches) were controlling events. In this scene, both Banquo and Macbeth show how they have been affected by the predictions.

Banquo remembers the Witches' promises first and recalls that Macbeth 'hast it now: King, Cawdor, Glamis' (line 1). He concludes that Macbeth 'playedst most foully for't' (line 3). He keeps his thoughts to himself and immediately considers the prophecies for his children, speculating that the prophecies might be his 'oracles as well' (line 9). If Banquo is wholly good, why does he not share his thoughts with others? We can only conclude that he has an interest in keeping quiet.

GLOSSARY		
4	**stand ... posterity**	continue in your family
s.d.	*Sennet*	a set of notes played on the trumpet
13	**all-thing**	totally
14	**solemn**	ceremonious
21	**still**	always
	grave and prosperous	weighty and profitable
56	**chid**	challenged
62	**unlineal**	outside my family
64	**issue**	descendants
78	**made good**	explained
80	**borne in hand**	deceived
	crossed	tricked
92–3	**hounds ... demi-wolves**	different breeds of dogs
93	**clept**	called
119	**avouch**	justify
133	**rubs nor botches**	flaws or mistakes
135	**material**	important
139	**straight**	immediately

CHECK THE BOOK A03

The 'reckless' (line 109) semi-professional murderer, seen here in the murderers hired by Macbeth is a stock figure in Jacobean drama, as is the contract killer in modern crime fiction on TV and in film. Bosola in John Webster's *The Dutchess of Malfi* (1614) represents a fully developed Jacobean example.

ACT III SCENE 2

SUMMARY

- Lady Macbeth realises that the satisfaction she and Macbeth sought has not been achieved.
- She tries to reassure her husband and urges him to act cheerfully.
- Although Macbeth's thoughts are fixed on Banquo, he tells his wife only that she will approve of his deeds.

ANALYSIS

KEEPING SECRETS

Macbeth and Lady Macbeth's weakening relationship is revealed. They feel similarly about the situation (compare lines 4–7 and 19–22) but are unable to share their thoughts with each other and, by now, Macbeth has detached himself from his reliance on his wife and pursues his own course. It is remarkable that in the middle of this scene he can ask his wife to act pleasantly to Banquo when we know that Banquo, on his orders, will never return. His brutalised nature is evident in the cool 'Be innocent of the knowledge, dearest chuck, / Till thou applaud the deed' (lines 45–6). Significantly, he invokes the same powers of darkness and witchcraft as he called on earlier in Act II Scene 1, lines 51–60.

STUDY FOCUS: SCORCHING THE SNAKE **A01**

Shakespeare brilliantly captures both Macbeth's brutality and his fear for the future through one vividly expressed thought. In telling Lady Macbeth that they have 'scorched the snake' (line 13), Macbeth indicates that the 'snake' is wounded but is still dangerous and despite their weak attempt to kill it off, it will threaten them in the future. The snake can be interpreted as symbolic of Banquo and more generally the Witches' predictions concerning Banquo's children. We have an insight into Macbeth's mind at this point. He eats 'in fear' and sleeps 'in the affliction of these terrible dreams' (lines 17–18), and in this sense we may feel that it is Macbeth who has been 'scorched' by his own sin. He appears to want death and compares his lack of peace with Duncan's greater peace in death.

GLOSSARY		
4	**had**	gained
7	**doubtful**	apprehensive, insecure
9	**sorriest**	most miserable
22	**ecstasy**	delirium
25	**levy**	troops
27	**sleek o'er**	smooth
31	**Present him eminence**	honour him

ACT III SCENE 3

SUMMARY

- The Murderers wait for Banquo to return to the palace.
- The two Murderers are joined by a third, sent by Macbeth.
- Banquo is attacked and killed but Fleance escapes.
- The Murderers acknowledge that they have only partly succeeded in their task.

ANALYSIS

THE THIRD MURDERER

In this scene the only characters present are the Murderers and their intended victims. We are therefore privy to the unravelling of Macbeth's plan. The first Murderer asks the third, 'But who did bid thee join with us? (line 1). The answer being, 'Macbeth' (line 2). This leads us to ask, did Macbeth fail to trust the first two Murderers or did he want to make sure the job was carried out? It appears that by sending in a third person, the planned double murders of Banquo and Fleance have failed. The third Murderer asks, 'Who did strike out the light?' (line 19). The first Murderer suggests that this was part of the plan, but by sending further help to make sure that the job is done, Macbeth has, in fact, sown confusion and allowed Fleance to escape. What does this tell us about his qualities as king? The state of Scotland under Macbeth's reign is one of confusion. We wonder about Macbeth's state of mind. Is he afraid of failure at this point? Is he indecisive? Does he give slightly different instructions to the third Murderer, which have unwittingly resulted in a very different outcome?

MACBETH'S MISTAKES

With the escape of Fleance, Macbeth's scheme has failed in a spectacular way. He has increased suspicions of his villainy, and the Witches' prophecy, which he had hoped to cancel, is still there to torment him. It is painfully ironic that according to the prophecy Banquo was not the real danger, the real danger was Banquo's son, Fleance, and yet Banquo is dead and Fleance has escaped. At the same time, Macbeth's already overwhelmed conscience is further pressed under the weight of another murder he knows to be indefensible.

GLOSSARY		
2	**He ... mistrust** there is no reason for us to distrust him (the newcomer)	
10	**within ... expectation** on the list of expected guests	
11	**about** the long way round (to the stables)	
21	**Best ... affair** the more important part of the job, or the larger part of the reward	

CRITICAL VIEWPOINT A02

Scene 3 opens half way through a conversation and at the close of Macbeth's speech to the murderers (III.1.138) he suggests he will 'Come to you anon' – we, however, are not privy to that conversation. Half-heard conversations and missing details add to the **Gothic** suspense of the play, and to the shadowy nature of events.

CONTEXT A04

Shakespeare's audience would have known that Fleance's escape not only fulfilled the Witches' prophecies but also was a compliment to King James I since James could trace his ancestry back to Banquo.

ACT III SCENE 4

SUMMARY

- Macbeth and Lady Macbeth welcome guests to their banquet.
- Macbeth is informed of Banquo's death and is also told of Fleance's escape.
- At the feast Macbeth is haunted by the ghost of Banquo.
- Lady Macbeth informs the guests that Macbeth is suffering from an illness he has had since he was a child.
- Macbeth decides to revisit the Witches.

ANALYSIS

THE BANQUET

This, the halfway point in the play, is a central scene in the analysis of Macbeth's career in crime. The newly established king holds a lavish feast to show his authority. At the beginning of the scene we have the ceremony of guests, hosts and civilised order interrupted by the sly appearance of one of Macbeth's hired killers. Macbeth's facade of decency begins to break down and it is clear that underneath this show there lurks a murderous heart. The appearance of Banquo's ghost is a poignant reminder of Macbeth's wickedness. We could argue that the ghost is the externalised form of Macbeth's guilt and fear of discovery, and although invisible to the other guests, is a terrifying reality to Macbeth himself. His wife loyally and resourcefully tries to protect him and shake him out of his obsession but, as she says, Macbeth is 'quite unmanned in folly' (line 72). Macbeth, a man celebrated for his courage in battle, cringes before the creation of his troubled conscience.

AFTER THE GHOST

When the ghost and the guests have gone, Macbeth's mind is not restored to calmness or repentance or even full trust in his wife. He can see no way out of his dilemma but by crushing everyone around him who questions his will. Fate, including the Witches, must be bullied into obedience. This is the final appearance of a sane Lady Macbeth. Her iron self-control, loyalty to her husband, apparent callousness – all evident in this scene – are qualities she still possesses. However, as we shall see, she has paid dearly for them.

STUDY FOCUS: SHAKESPEARE'S GHOSTS `A03`

Ghosts are not uncommon in Shakespeare's plays. Apart from their dramatic impact, their use seems to suggest an interest in the circumstances and psychology that might give rise to their appearance. In this scene, nobody but Macbeth sees the ghost of Banquo. This might suggest that the ghost is a figment of his guilt-stricken imagination. This is in contrast to the ghost that Hamlet and his friends see at the beginning of the play *Hamlet*. For a discussion of what Shakespeare's audience might have believed about ghosts, read chapter 3 'Ghost or devil?' in J. Dover Wilson's *What Happens in Hamlet* (1955).

CHECK THE FILM `A03`

Reading the play rather than seeing it on stage or in a film version emphasises the sharp contrasts between the three main areas of the play's action: the private world of Macbeth's mind, the intimacy of his dialogue with Lady Macbeth, and the public activities such as this banquet. Roman Polanski's *Macbeth* (1971) makes these contrasts very clear, with several prolonged banqueting scenes.

REVISION FOCUS: TASK 2 A04

How far do you agree with the statements below?

- Macbeth's moral decline is due to his misuse of the Witches' prophecies.
- Banquo is as morally bankrupt as Macbeth because he also took notice of the Witches' prophecies.

Try writing opening paragraphs for essays based on the discussion points above.

KEY QUOTATION: ACT III SCENE 4 A01

Key quotation: 'I am in blood / Stepped in so far, that, should I wade no more, / Returning were as tedious as go o'er' (III.4.136–8).

- Shakespeare is saying here that Macbeth has involved himself in so many murders that it is as easy for him to carry on than to turn back.
- Macbeth compares his course of action with wading across a river of blood, creating a vivid image of his bloody reign.
- The word 'tedious' reveals the hardening of Macbeth's heart.

GLOSSARY

1–2	**At first / And last** from beginning to end	
11	**Be large in mirth** enjoy yourselves	
18	**the nonpareil** without equal	
23	**cabined … bound in** imprisoned, confined	
70–2	**If charnel houses … kites** if tombs cannot hold down the dead we will need to have them eaten by birds of prey	
92	**Avaunt** away	
123	**Augurs** prophecies, connections in nature	

CONTEXT A04

In lines 32–6 'The feast … without it', Macbeth is suggesting that unless repeated welcomes are given by the host, a feast becomes like a paid-for meal. The food itself is better at home but outside one expects more ceremony to make the meal worthwhile.

CONTEXT A04

Macbeth asks his guests to 'know your own degrees' (line 1). In Shakespeare's time, the guests would take their places at a long table according to their ranks and titles. Those with the highest ranks and titles would be considered the most important guests and would sit closest to the king. In our own day, those with the most important jobs in government sit closest to the prime minister at the cabinet table.

EXTENDED COMMENTARY

ACT III SCENE 4 LINES 82–143

The passage comes from a scene which is, for most of the time, crowded with people. In the final twenty lines, Macbeth and Lady Macbeth are on their own. The opening of the scene shows Macbeth as the masterful and hospitable king: the banquet, because we have not seen his coronation at Scone, is a formal confirmation of his status. The first twelve lines emphasise welcome and order but a different note is struck in line 13: 'There's blood upon thy face!' This disquieting note is reiterated and magnified with the appearance, to Macbeth, of Banquo's ghost. The particular passage under discussion occurs after the disappearance of the ghost and focuses on Macbeth and how he copes with the appearance of Banquo, who has just been murdered on his instructions. Towards the end of the passage Macbeth declares his intention to seek out the Witches and, as if he has conjured them, they immediately appear in the following scene (Act III Scene 5).

Whatever theory we may have about ghosts, the appearance of Banquo is real to Macbeth – as only he sees it. What most frightens him is the unnaturalness of the thing; it is recognisably Banquo but it is dead: '**Thy bones are marrowless, thy blood is cold. / Thou hast no speculation in those eyes**' (lines 93–4). If he could fight physically with it, he would not be afraid, but it is a 'horrible shadow', an 'Unreal mockery'. Macbeth's guilt and imagination combine to see the ghost as an unstoppable force of vengeance. Even after it has disappeared, he sees it in a paranoid way, believing that it is seeking him out, with the help of natural agents (lines 121–5). His emphasis on 'man' works in two senses: 'man' as human and 'man' as male. The second sense recalls his wife's taunts in Act I Scene 7 and it is she, in the present scene, who first challenges his manhood: '**Are you a man?**' (line 57) and '**What, quite unmanned in folly?**' (line 72). As happened in the earlier scene, she has to cajole and organise him through his difficulties – in both scenes she appears more composed, more in control.

Macbeth is thrown into complete confusion so that he no longer is sure who or what he is (lines 111–12). After Lady Macbeth has ushered out the guests, Macbeth has to reassert himself and in his speech in lines 129–39 he speaks as if to himself. The word 'I' is repeated nine times and his wife seems excluded till the 'we' in line 141. In the speech he shakes off his fears and irresolution and proclaims an extreme line of action: '**For mine own good / All causes shall give way**' (lines 134–5). In the final lines of the scene his confidence has returned and he seems to laugh off the business with the ghost as simple inexperience in crime, something he aims to sort out very soon, after seeking the advice of the Witches.

The initial disorder, however, and Macbeth's frantic efforts to restore conviviality, '**I drink to the general joy o'the whole table**' (line 88), reveal the hollowness of Macbeth's hospitality. Macbeth is shown to be ill, '**he grows worse and worse**' (line 116), and his disorder is reflected in how he sees nature: '**Stones have been known to move and trees to speak**' (line 122). There is a reiteration in the vocabulary of this disorder: 'infirmity', '**spoils**', '**tremble**', '**Unreal**', '**displaced**', '**broke**', '**disorder**', '**overcome**', '**at odds**', '**lack**' and '**self-abuse**'. There is also a strand of imagery that relates to blood and bloodlessness.

The blood which symbolises Banquo's murder obsesses Macbeth throughout the scene. Even the ghost's hair seems 'gory' when he first appears and his second appearance comes immediately after Macbeth's call: 'Give me some wine; fill full!' (line 87). The redness of blood and the paleness of the ghost indicate a

CRITICAL VIEWPOINT **A02**

Essentially, it could be argued that this scene emphasises Macbeth's further reliance on the Witches, which brings about his inevitable destruction.

contrast between life and death and, in the passage, a conflict between the two: 'blood will have blood' (line 121); it is as if Banquo's ghost has come to seek Macbeth's blood. Lady Macbeth's cheeks are seen to have their 'natural ruby' and Macbeth's are 'blanched with fear' (lines 114–15). He is the only one to have seen the ghost. Macbeth, as the murderer, becomes the 'man of blood' and he sees himself wading in blood.

In the passage, the speech of the attendant lords is mechanical, dutiful, predictable and minimal. Lady Macbeth's function is to rescue her husband and re-establish some normality. Her pieces of dialogue are short and to the point, a series of statements and urgent requests. The urgency is most apparent in her longest speech (lines 116–19) where her three and a half lines are broken into six terse units, culminating in a desperate or rude command: 'But go at once'. Macbeth's speech is much more varied, as he struggles to regain control of himself and come to terms with what has taken place. His struggle is obvious in the opening speech of the passage where, in his rush to sound normal, he becomes almost incoherent. Lines 86–91 are made up of jerky phrases, reflecting his upset mind. For example, in line 90 he exclaims 'we thirst' when he means 'we drink', and he ends his toast with the circular 'And all to all'. His speech is marked with exclamations and questions. His impassioned, fevered address to the ghost, invisible to all but himself, conveys his confusion and guilt. When Ross demands, 'What sights, my lord?' (line 115), Lady Macbeth intervenes quickly to prevent her husband from further incriminating himself. Macbeth often speaks in parallel phrases as if making stabs at understanding what he finds incomprehensible. He pulls himself back towards normality with his question, 'What is the night?' (line 125), and his **syntax** calms down into dogged determination in lines 131–9.

It is significant that in lines 82 and 95, Lady Macbeth speaks the second half of a line as if she is frightened to let her husband continue; she diverts the proceedings. Generally, the verse follows an **iambic** pentameter pattern and the metre has no obvious peculiarities or lapses. An oddity does take place in the final ten lines. Macbeth departs from the **blank verse** (unrhymed) to speak in rhyming couplets. It is worth noting that Macbeth sometimes does move into rhyme throughout the play. In this instance he has just mentioned the Witches and they habitually speak in rhymed couplets; a link does seem to exist between the Witches and Macbeth through his use of rhymed couplets. The use of rhymed couplets here gives a measured tread to Macbeth's resolve. He sounds hypnotised by something in his mind, something which he only half understands:

Strange things I have in head, that will to hand;
Which must be acted ere they may be scanned. (lines 138–9)

The rhyme, the regularity of the metre, and the balancing of the two halves of each line give a **rhetorical** assurance to his statement.

ACT III SCENE 5

SUMMARY

- Hecat meets the three Witches on the heath during a thunderstorm. She is angry with them because they have dealt with Macbeth without consulting her.
- She tells them to prepare for a meeting with Macbeth in the morning and predicts Macbeth's downfall.

ANALYSIS

HECAT

Hecat is 'the mistress of [the Witches'] charms' (line 6), but her anger towards them seems to stem mostly from the fact that they have helped a 'wayward son' (line 11). She realises that Macbeth was not interested in witchcraft but only concerned with what he could gain from meeting the Witches. Her demand that the Witches go back to 'Acheron' (line 15) – the river in Hell – and prepare spells is made with the purpose of entrapping Macbeth. She wants the Witches to conjure up apparitions which will lead him to his ruin. We are aware that Hecat, a more powerful force than the first three Witches, plans to bring about the downfall of Macbeth and we await the next act with anticipation.

THE WITCHES' LIMITATIONS

As in Act I Scene 3 we are again aware that the Witches have limitations to their powers. They have behaved like naughty children and acted without authority, their intention was to have fun and cause chaos. When we recall that a good king has been murdered and a good, loyal man has also been killed, we have little sympathy for their fun. The Witches initially picked out Macbeth's character flaw – ambition. They played on his flaw to bring about a state of confusion and chaos in Scotland. To restore order they would have to bring about Macbeth's downfall and death. However, they are no longer in charge of events – Hecat is now directing their deeds.

STUDY FOCUS: THE USE OF RHYMING COUPLETS   A02

Many scholars doubt whether this scene was written by Shakespeare. In its **imagery** and attitude to Macbeth, however, it fits easily into the rest of the play. The wild determination obvious in Macbeth at the end of Scene 4 is remarked on by Hecat. Although Shakespeare has used rhyming couplets throughout the play, often to end scenes, this is the only time a character has spoken a monologue in rhyming couplets. This difference in style adds fuel to those who believe the scene was not written by Shakespeare. This scene, like the Porter's scene (II.3), is different in tone to the rest of the play.

GLOSSARY		
2	**beldam**	an old woman, especially a malicious one, a hag
3	**Saucy**	impudent
21	**Unto a dismal**	preparing for a disastrous
26	**sleights**	arts
30	**spurn**	ignore

GRADE BOOSTER   A02

It's important that you know the difference between a monologue and a **soliloquy**. A monologue is an extended and uninterrupted speech by a character in drama. A soliloquy, on the other hand, is the expression of a character's innermost thoughts and feelings. A soliloquy is usually expressed to the audience without addressing other characters. In this scene, Hecat is delivering a monologue.

CONTEXT   A03

Hecat was the Greek goddess of witchcraft, sorcery and the dead. She is perhaps an odd addition to the Christian world of *Macbeth*. The fairies in *A Midsummer Night's Dream* owe her allegiance but they are mischievous rather than malevolent. In this scene in *Macbeth*, Hecat is clearly malevolent and plans Macbeth's destruction.

ACT III SCENE 6

SUMMARY

- Events are reported through the conversation between Lennox and an unnamed lord.
- Lennox examines the recent 'accidents' and realises that Macbeth is responsible for the murders of Duncan and Banquo.
- Macbeth has sent a rebuke to Macduff for his absence at the feast while Macduff has gone to England to rouse support against Macbeth.
- There is growing opposition to Macbeth.

ANALYSIS

LENNOX'S PERSPECTIVE ON EVENTS

Although this scene follows immediately on from the previous one, we are given a sense of a stretch of time and, just as at the end of Act II, a larger perspective on events. The sense of Macbeth's tyranny, resembling that of a modern police state, is communicated acutely in Lennox's analysis of what has happened. His words are ironic, oblique and somewhat guarded, even if the implication of his remarks is quite clear. Macbeth is using spies and Lennox is unable to speak openly. He has obviously spoken to others on previous occasions, hinting at how the deaths lead back to Macbeth. Shakespeare has chosen not to give us these conversations, but we soon grasp that people are talking – and putting two and two together.

MACBETH'S GRIP ON SCOTLAND

We learn that Macbeth is trying to tighten his hold on the country but the opposition is difficult to pin down and the English king, 'most pious Edward' (line 27), is prepared to help against Macbeth. We have an insight into how Macbeth runs his country when a lord mentions to Lennox that the people need meat and sleep – that everyone wants to eat and sleep without fear of the threat of murder. It is quite obvious that Macbeth is acting as a tyrant. Lennox believes that an English army, freeing Scotland of Macbeth, would be a blessing. He calls Scotland a 'suffering country' (line 48). This is something Macbeth himself will recognise later on in the play.

STUDY FOCUS: MACDUFF'S OPPOSITION A02

Macduff entered the play after the murder of Duncan, so we expect him to be detached from Macbeth. From his refusal to see Macbeth crowned at Scone and to attend the banquet, it would appear that he has been suspicious of Macbeth from the moment he entered the castle at Forres.

A hint of Macduff's approaching tragedy is evident in the last few lines where the messenger, realising that Macduff is refusing to obey Macbeth's express orders, feels that Macduff will 'rue the time / That clogs me with this answer' (lines 42–3).

GLOSSARY		
2	**Which ... further**	and you can draw your own conclusions
8	**want the thought**	fail to think
13	**thralls**	slaves
28–9	**malevolence ... respect**	his misfortunes lessen the high honour given to him

CRITICAL VIEWPOINT A04

This lurid scene shows Shakespeare (perhaps) participating in this general superstitious outcry. Is he perhaps reflecting the views of the time back to the audience, like a mirror, so that they can see themselves? Or is he acting like a social commentator?

CONTEXT A04

Some of Edward the Confessor's contemporaries believed that he spent too much time in prayer. They thought he should have spent longer running his country than trying to save his own soul and he was nicknamed Holy Ned.

ACT IV SCENE 1

SUMMARY

- The Witches make their charm.
- Macbeth seeks out the Witches. He sees the three apparitions and is filled with confidence.
- He is given the news of Macduff's flight to England.
- He decides to murder Macduff's family.

ANALYSIS

FALSE PROPHECIES

The Witches' broth is made as unpleasant and unnatural as possible to prepare the audience's minds for the arrival of Macbeth. There is a parallel between the wickedness practised by the Witches and that practised by Macbeth. Significantly, Macbeth addresses the Witches almost familiarly and he 'conjures' them in their own manner, showing his identification with their evil ways. The fact that the three prophecies – warning Macbeth against Macduff, telling him that he cannot be harmed by one 'of woman born' (line 17) and guaranteeing his safety until Birnan Wood comes to Dunsinane Hill – will prove to be false and that their purpose is to trick him is now evident to the audience and heightens the sense of inevitable doom.

STUDY FOCUS: SYMBOLIC APPARITIONS   A02

The Apparitions are obviously symbolic. The most straightforward interpretation sees the figures as: 1) prophetic of the killed Macbeth; 2) the infant Macduff; and 3) young Malcolm coming to Dunsinane. Macbeth, typically, wishes to accept the Witches' favourable predictions and to reject what is awkward for him. In the same vein, it can be argued that his horror at Banquo's ghost has much to do with his sense of powerlessness to prevent Banquo's family eventually succeeding to the throne. When Macbeth insists, the Witches conjure up a line of kings that, to Macbeth, appear to 'stretch out to th' crack of doom' (line 116). His impotent rage expresses itself in the plan to massacre Macduff's family.

REVISION FOCUS: TASK 3   A02

How far do you agree with the statements below?

- The violent descriptions and bleak settings enhance the Gothic tone of the play.
- Shakespeare uses contrasting settings to build and sustain dramatic tension.

Try writing opening paragraphs for essays based on the discussion points above.

GLOSSARY

1	**brinded**	streaky coloured
3	**Harpier**	spirit of the witch
28	**eclipse**	associated with catastrophes
31	**Ditch-delivered**	born in a ditch
	drab	prostitute
116	**crack of doom**	the Last Day/Day of Judgement
146	**firstlings**	first impulses

CONTEXT   A04

In 1603, spurred on by James I's obsession with witchcraft, parliament passed a law against 'invocation or conjuration of any evil or wicked spirit'. It specified that no one should 'take up any dead man, woman or child out of the grave, – or the skin, bone, or any part of the dead person, to be employed or used in any manner of witchcraft, sorcery, charm or enchantment'.

CONTEXT   A04

The show of eight kings are all ancestors of James I, from Banquo's line down to James' grandfather. Shakespeare does not show the queen, James' mother. She was Mary Queen of Scots and not a popular figure in English eyes. James came to the throne after the death of his mother. According to historians, he did little to prevent her death.

ACT IV SCENE 2

SUMMARY

- Ross informs Lady Macduff of her husband's flight to England and she fears that her husband has left her unprotected.
- She finds his desertion of his family hard to justify and discusses the situation with her young son.
- A stranger arrives and warns them to escape immediately.
- Lady Macduff and her son are murdered.

ANALYSIS

TYRANNY UNLEASHED

This scene contains a moving portrayal of a family on the brink of a terrible atrocity. Lady Macduff and her son are presented to us as pathetically vulnerable. The futility of Lady Macduff's condemnation of her husband's unexplained departure heightens our sense of her political innocence, while Ross and the Messenger, fresh from the court of Macbeth, know how tyranny operates and how the individual has to act secretly to survive. The glib cleverness of her young son has the same **pathos**. We know that Macbeth's agents are on their way and the discussion between mother and son is wasted breath.

MACDUFF'S SON

Macduff's son is witty and clever. He is a boy full of potential, which makes it more poignant that he is about to die. He is also brave, calling the first Murderer a 'shag-haired villain' (line 83). The last words of the poor boy indicate that he has rare qualities – he is thinking only of his mother when he cries 'Run away, I pray you' (line 85). His brutal murder should fill us with horror and through it Shakespeare shows us Macbeth's further descent into tyranny.

MACBETH AS TYRANT

Macbeth now believes he is invincible and the murder of Macduff's wife and children appears to be out of spite. Over a period of time, he has become a very different person from the man who contemplated and agonised over the killing of Duncan. He is now willing to order the deaths of innocent people – seemingly without remorse.

GLOSSARY		
7	**titles** property	
14	**cuz** form of 'cousin'	
15	**school** control	
17	**fits o'the season** uncertainties of the time	
48	**swears and lies** swears an oath (promise) and then breaks it	
81	**unsanctified** unprotected	
84	**fry** offspring	

CRITICAL VIEWPOINT A03

Lady Macduff states that her husband lacks the instinct that even a wren would have in protecting its young. Lady Macduff's condemnation of her husband's motives is reminiscent of Lady Macbeth's attack on her husband (I.7). We could argue that the women's assaults on their husband's characters are equally false, but in tragically opposite ways (see IV.3).

GRADE BOOSTER A03

When comparing texts, it is worth remembering that stories in *The Bloody Chamber* deal with murders of innocent people. The Marquis has killed his wives and wishes to kill another. 'Puss-in-Boots', a story from the collection, is about the murder of an 'innocent' old man. The theme of revenge is also present in *The White Devil*, *Frankenstein* and *Wuthering Heights*.

CONTEXT A04

In Greek tragedy, violence, such as Oedipus putting out his eyes, happened off stage. The Latin word *obscenus*, from which our word 'obscene' is derived, means 'off stage'. Violence and sensationalism were common in the Elizabethan and Jacobean theatre. Shakespeare's most violent play is *Titus Andronicus* (1593), which features chopped-off hands and heads, and the eating of a pie made with human flesh, as well as numerous murders.

ACT IV SCENE 3

SUMMARY

- Malcolm and Macduff meet at the court of the English king.
- Malcolm is suspicious of Macduff and tests him.
- Macduff is informed that an army is ready to fight Macbeth.
- He learns of the slaughter of his family, and vows revenge on Macbeth.

ANALYSIS

UNITING THE FORCES AGAINST MACBETH

This scene is longer and slower moving than any other scene in this play. Its main function is to assemble and assess the moral forces present in the drama before the final attack on Macbeth is launched. The corrupt Macbeth is destroying Scotland and Malcolm and Macduff need to unite to purge the country of a leader put on the throne by the Witches' machinations.

MALCOLM'S SUITABILITY AS KING

In the safety of King Edwards' palace, Macduff is able to describe the horrors of Macbeth's reign. There is **dramatic irony** at work here as we know Macduff is not yet aware of the full horrors – the brutal murder of his own family. Malcolm, presumably afraid of assassination, queries Macduff's political integrity. To test Macduff, he presents a picture of himself as worse than Macbeth. This depiction of himself, together with his denial of all the regal virtues, offers by negatives a definition of the duties of kingship. We can see that Malcolm will be a good king and that he will restore order to a disunited Scotland. This reinforces the picture we already have in our minds concerning Malcolm as a very different ruler to Macbeth (see I.4.3–12).

MACDUFF'S REACTION

Macduff blames himself for the death of his wife and children. At first he is inconsolable. It is Malcolm who persuades him that he should 'Dispute it like a man' (line 219). Thus the murders further galvanise Macduff to face Macbeth and kill him – he wants revenge and it appears that Macbeth, who was told to beware Macduff, has now given him the spur to 'Bring … this fiend of Scotland' (line 232) to within a sword's length. We await the final act with anticipation.

GLOSSARY		
3	**mortal**	deadly
4	**Bestride ... birthdom**	defend our fallen native land
8	**Like ... dolour**	the same cry of sorrow
19–20	**recoil ... charge**	do something wicked if ordered to by the king
78	**staunchless**	limitless
88	**foisons**	plenty
174	**nice**	elaborate
217	**hell-kite**	bird of prey from hell
225	**demerits**	sins

CONTEXT A04

In his history plays and tragedies, Shakespeare often dwells on the appalling consequences of civil war. Showing the murder of a small child on stage is a sensational and terrible reminder of such a disaster.

CHECK THE FILM A03

This whole scene, in which Macduff is tested by Malcolm in the English court, is left out of Roman Polanski's *Macbeth* (1971). At the end of Polanski's film, Donalbain visits the Witches' coven. Polanski's film interpretation is that Donalbain will become like Macbeth. There is nothing in the text to suggest that Donalbain will act as Polanski suggests – but it is an interesting interpretation. The text suggests Malcolm is more like his parents, as he has strong principles and virtues and qualities that Macbeth never had, so we can be assured that his kingship will be sound.

EXTENDED COMMENTARY

ACT IV SCENE 3 LINES 31–100

These lines occur in the longest scene in *Macbeth,* and the first half of the scene poses problems for any production because it is so static and seems, in its length, out of proportion to the rest of a very busy play. The scene, the only one set outside Scotland, sits between two of the most theatrical scenes in the play: the murder of Macduff's family and Lady Macbeth's sleepwalking. It offers views on Macbeth and the action surrounding him from a perspective outside that situation. We see Malcolm as an aspiring king opposed to Macbeth; we see King Edward of England as a saintly and beneficent ruler, a healer in contrast to Macbeth; and we see Macduff's grief as genuine and not political. When we read the discussion between Malcolm and Macduff we are still horrified at the butchery of Macduff's family which we have witnessed but of which Macduff is still ignorant; and, when we are reading or seeing the play for a second time, we can anticipate the mental collapse of Lady Macbeth in the following scene.

The passage, which takes the form of a conversation between Macduff and Malcolm, begins with the patriotic despondency of Macduff, 'Bleed, bleed, poor country!', and closes on a similar note, 'O Scotland, Scotland!' Although the younger man, Malcolm, takes the initiative and establishes the terms of the discussion, the lines are shared fairly evenly. The passage moves through a series of problems posed by Malcolm and attempts at some solution or accommodation by Macduff. Malcolm gradually increases the challenge until Macduff can offer no more flexibility and declares his hopes defeated. In Malcolm's subsequent speech (lines 114–37), he completely

overthrows the conclusion of our passage, and admits the truth – that he is virtuous.

In the lines leading up to line 31, Macduff, although more impetuous than Malcolm, is forced to defend himself: 'I am not treacherous' (line 18) and 'I have lost my hopes' (line 24). He is hurt that Malcolm can question his sincerity and prepares to leave (line 34). Malcolm has a measured, rehearsed way of speaking (see the balanced phrases of lines 8–10) which offends Macduff but there are reasonable grounds for Malcolm's suspicions: why has Macduff left his family undefended if he so detests Macbeth? If, as he claims, Macduff has deserted and defied Macbeth out of love for his country, how far will he go to replace Macbeth? Malcolm tests him by presenting himself as more evil than the tyrannical Macbeth and as determined to ruin Scotland even further. Macduff, so eager for Macbeth to be deposed, tries to accommodate the claimed wickedness of Malcolm, believing that he cannot possibly be worse. When Malcolm finally persuades him of his villainy, Macduff breaks from him in despair. Macduff emerges from the test as an honest, patriotic idealist, flexible only up to a point. We see his idealism as brave but futile because we know what he does not, that his defenceless family has already been massacred.

By Shakespearean standards elsewhere in this play and in other plays, the **imagery** in this passage is neither dense nor very striking. The most obvious line of imagery presents Scotland as a suffering body which can bleed, weep and be weakened by wounds. The sickness and suffering of Scotland are caused by the wickedness of Macbeth. This is in direct contrast with the caring and curative powers of King Edward in England – Edward being described as 'good' and 'full of grace'. A second line of

GRADE BOOSTER A01

Remember to think about how different scenes would appear on stage. This seems a very ordinary part of the play: two men, Malcolm and Macduff, are talking and there is no action. Nobody enters or exits. The **blank verse** is regular and there are no abrupt shifts or interruptions. No voice is raised and there are no stage directions.

CONTEXT A04

'O Scotland, Scotland!' (IV.3.100). For the Londoners seeing the play, Scotland would likely seem a foreign country, one often at war with England and several days of difficult journey from the English capital.

CONTEXT A04

Shakespeare's source for *Macbeth* (Holinshed's *Chronicles of England, Scotland and Ireland*, first published in 1577, reprinted in an expanded edition in 1587) describes Edward the Confessor curing people ill with the King's Evil (scrofula) by touch. Shakespeare may have included this passage to flatter James I, who believed that he also had this healing power.

CRITICAL VIEWPOINT A03

Be aware of links and connections within the text. Sickness is a thematic image used throughout *Macbeth*. Try considering this passage in relation to the doctor's role in the last act.

imagery presents the alleged faults in Malcolm as growths or plants. In lines 51–2 he claims, 'All the particulars of vice [are] so grafted / That, when they shall be opened', that is, when they shall blossom, they shall produce incomparable nastiness. In lines 76–7 he says that his greed 'grows / In my most ill-composed affection', perhaps with a pun on compost, and Macduff continues this image in line 85 when he worries that Malcolm's greed 'Sticks deeper, grows with more pernicious root'. Individual images tend to be rather clichéd: 'yoke' (line 39), 'pure as snow' (line 53), 'lamb' (line 54),

'cistern of my lust' (line 63) and 'vulture' (line 74). The single unusual image occurs when Malcolm says: 'had I power, I should / Pour the sweet milk of concord into hell' (lines 97–8). It recalls 'the milk of human-kindness' (I.5.15), 'take my milk for gall' (I.5.46) and 'the babe that milks me' (I.7.55), all in speeches by Lady Macbeth. As in these, the milk here symbolises innocence, humanness and nourishment. Malcolm threatens to exterminate human decency and order and replace them with anarchy and animosity – of course, he is testing Macduff.

Unlike the passage in the extended commentary for Act II Scene 4 lines 82–143, this passage has very little abruptness or suddenness. The two men speak in turn, say what they wish to say, and do not interrupt each other. There are few exclamations or questions; one statement by Malcolm is matched with a counter-statement from Macduff. Both men, but particularly Malcolm, tend to speak in substantial sentences. More than half the lines are un-end-stopped as if the characters have thought out carefully what they wish to say. Malcolm uses 'I' fourteen times and 'my' twelve times; Macduff uses 'I' only once. Macduff tries to see in general terms what Malcolm says very personally. He tries to defuse or accommodate Malcolm's claims of depravity. Although he claims to be a person with no self-discipline, Malcolm speaks in a rational, coherent manner. An example of his rationality is his use of lists: first of bad characteristics in lines 57–9 with eight qualities, and second of good characteristics in lines 92–4 with twelve qualities.

Sometimes the verse is not dynamic and lines and groups of lines can sound very prosaic. The rhythm is unpronounced for the most part, and the sound of the verse does not draw attention to itself; the concentration is on the debate between Malcolm and Macduff. We are made to listen to the argument without diversions or distractions. The frequency of run-on lines and the total lack of rhyme further undermine the individual line as a unit of verse. Each speech is like a paragraph which we have to hear whole.

CHECK THE BOOK A03

There are many passages in Shakespeare's history plays dwelling on the nature of kingship. For a comparison with this scene in *Macbeth*, examine *Henry IV Part 1*, Act III Scene 2, in which King Henry rebukes his son Prince Harry for his unkingly behaviour with Sir John Falstaff.

ACT V SCENE 1

SUMMARY

- Lady Macbeth's lady-in-waiting has sent for a doctor.
- The doctor and the lady-in-waiting watch to see if Lady Macbeth walks in her sleep.
- Lady Macbeth refers to the deaths of Duncan, Macduff's wife and Banquo.
- The doctor confesses that he is incapable of dealing with such cases.

ANALYSIS

THE MENTAL DECLINE OF LADY MACBETH

We have not seen Lady Macbeth since Act III Scene 4 and her behaviour in the present scene shows that her carefully contrived mask has slipped. Now, alone, her loyalty to her husband remains intact; only once does she reproach him: 'no more o'that. You mar all with this starting' (line 43). Her behaviour reveals that she has given all and now her present is overwhelmed by the past, 'What's done cannot be undone' (lines 63–4).

Frantically, she mimes washing her hands, 'Out, damned spot' (line 34), and 'What, will these hands ne'er be clean?' (line 42). The words she speaks in this scene are the opposite to her words after the death of Duncan, when she sought to control her husband, 'A little water clears us of this deed' (II.2.67). Clearly, her control has broken down and she is being destroyed through guilt. Her ramblings suggest that she feels responsible for Macbeth's actions after the murder of Duncan, 'The Thane of Fife had a wife; where is she now?' (line 41). In her derangement, Lady Macbeth speaks in prose, as do Shakespeare's other characters who are driven into madness, such as Ophelia in *Hamlet*, or King Lear.

Lady Macbeth has repressed most of the fears and guilt she has during her waking life, and it seems that these have come to haunt her during her sleeping life. Nature has hit back at a time when Lady Macbeth's conscious mind is not on the alert and we are reminded that she also repressed her womanly nature – 'Unsex me here' (I.5.39). Perhaps her nervous energy has been exhausted, or the evil spirits she requested in Act I Scene 5 have done their worst and now left her.

THE ROLE OF THE DOCTOR

The conversation between the Doctor and the Gentlewoman allows us to understand Lady Macbeth's movements, actions and thoughts. The Doctor is fully aware that Lady Macbeth has unwittingly confessed to the murder of Duncan and is amazed to hear that the rumours are true. He concludes that 'Unnatural deeds / Do breed unnatural troubles' (lines 67–8), another example of a commoner remarking on the unnaturalness of events. In his medical capacity, the doctor is aware that Lady Macbeth might commit suicide and instructs the Gentlewoman to 'Remove … all means of annoyance' (line 72). Unfortunately we are aware that there is no hope of removing the cause of her discomfort and this prepares us for her death in Scene 5.

GLOSSARY		
4	**field**	fighting
50	**sorely charged**	heavily burdened
52	**dignity**	worth
67	**abroad**	about
74	**mated**	bewildered

> **GRADE BOOSTER** A03
>
> To achieve the best grades at AS and A2, you will need to understand how some features of *Macbeth* are part of the **Gothic** genre. The setting and atmosphere in this scene are gloomy, while secrets and conspiracy lurk beneath the surface, and Lady Macbeth descends into madness – an aspect common to the Gothic genre. Think of the madwoman in the attic in *Jane Eyre* and Lucy's inability to sleep in *Dracula*.

ACT V SCENE 2

SUMMARY

- The Scottish nobles go to Birnam Wood to join Malcolm's English army.
- Donalbain is not with the English forces.
- Macbeth is becoming more desperate and support is deserting him.
- Only mercenaries stand with Macbeth.

ANALYSIS

EVENTS MOVE QUICKLY

A series of short scenes gives the impression of swift action and manoeuvring armies. Macbeth is being gradually isolated by his opponents. Even his wife is shown to have collapsed under the pressure. As the besieging force strengthens, Macbeth is left more and more on his own. The description of him is parallel to the isolated picture of his wife in the previous scene. Earlier in the play, when he knew he was unfit to be king, he described himself as being dressed in borrowed robes; here, Macbeth's title is described as hanging 'loose about him, like a giant's robe / Upon a dwarfish thief' (lines 21–2). The clothing **imagery** implies that he is unfit for kingship and should be removed from the throne as soon as possible.

STUDY FOCUS: AN ILLNESS OF THE MIND? `A02`

Cathness reports to Menteth that some claim Macbeth is mad. He understands that Macbeth is unable to 'buckle his distempered cause / Within the belt of rule' (lines 15–16) meaning he cannot govern his frenzied behaviour. Here a connection is made between the unruliness of Macbeth's mind and his kingdom: both are beyond his control. The report about Macbeth's behaviour, observed as if he is an outsider, is a link to the previous scene – where the Doctor and the Gentlewoman observe Lady Macbeth. The behaviour of both is linked to madness. Throughout this scene we are aware of doctor and patient imagery such as 'medicine', 'sickly' and 'purged' (lines 27–8). Is it possible to claim that both Macbeth and his wife are suffering from mental illness, having killed the rightful king?

CRITICAL VIEWPOINT `A02`

The narrative structure of the short scenes in Act V give us the effect of the stir and bustle of a battlefield. Although the action has not yet started, we are mentally prepared for action. The successive scenes take us alternatively to each set of combatants. Macbeth is, in effect, entrenched but the English army have comparative space.

GLOSSARY

s.d.	*colours*	banners
10	**unrough**	beardless
15	**buckle ... cause**	keep control of his disorderly forces
18	**upbraid**	rebuke
	faith-breach	treachery
19	**sovereign flower**	King Malcolm

ACT V SCENE 3

SUMMARY

- Macbeth is besieged in Dunsinane Castle.
- He still trusts the Witches' predictions even while hearing of the English army's approach.
- He despairs of finding a cure for his wife.

ANALYSIS

MACBETH'S ERRATIC BEHAVIOUR

Macbeth has become violent and inconsistent with his servants, his conduct and speech are wild. He repeats and contradicts himself and does not seem able to listen properly to what others say. When the Doctor tells him about Lady Macbeth, he seems more concerned with a cure for his own situation than with a treatment for his wife. But behind the shouting, Macbeth realises that he is coming to the end of his resources, nobody is freely loyal to him and his behaviour prevents him from considering his situation calmly and realistically. The Doctor's diagnosis of Lady Macbeth's condition gives Macbeth no comfort but he asks the Doctor to find a remedy for Scotland's situation. He shows his determination to fight to the end.

STUDY FOCUS: TIRED OF LIFE `A01`

This scene shows Macbeth's bitterness and at this point it is difficult to have sympathy with him. Rather, we must see his life as a warning to any would-be usurper. It is very clear that Macbeth has gained nothing by obtaining the crown. He has grown tired of life and feels the best has gone. In his short **soliloquy** he believes his life 'is fallen into the sere, the yellow leaf' (line 23) and we are led to conclude that the murders have not brought him or Lady Macbeth any happiness. He knows that, as an older man, he will not have 'honour, love, obedience, troops of friend' (line 25). His state of mind can be judged if we look closely at lines 47–56. Macbeth asks the attendant to put on his armour, moments later he asks for it to be pulled off. Finally, he asks for the servant to follow him with the armour. Macbeth is not thinking clearly – as a soldier, he must know he is beaten and his agitation must be great.

KEY QUOTATION: ACT V SCENE 3 `A01`

Key quotation: 'I have lived long enough: my way of life / Is fallen into the sere, the yellow leaf' (lines 22–3).

- Macbeth is saying that he has lost his reason for living. Life, for him, has lost its meaning and he feels it's withering and falling away like a yellow leaf in autumn.
- Macbeth is tired of living. He believes the best of life has passed by and he has nothing to look forward to in his life.

CRITICAL VIEWPOINT `A02`

In contrast to Lady Macbeth's incoherent ramblings, as Macbeth's situation grows more desperate, in this scene he is given some of the most memorable and exciting poetry in the play.

CHECK THE BOOK `A03`

Books by coaches aimed at actors often have great insights into the energy of Shakespeare's verse. See Cicely Berry's *The Actor and His Text* (1987) or Patsy Rodenburg's *Speaking Shakespeare* (2002).

GLOSSARY

1	**them**	the thanes
8	**epicures**	luxury lovers
12	**goose**	cowardly and stupid
15	**dis-seat**	unthrone
43	**oblivious antidote**	cure that makes one forget

CONTEXT A04

CONTEXT A04

There are biblical references throughout this **soliloquy** which the Jacobean audience would recognise. In the Book of Job Chapter 8, Job states that 'For we are but of yesterday, and are ignorant: for our days upon earth are but a shadow.' Whereas God allowed Satan to test Job, Macbeth has allied himself to evil. God rightfully restored Job but Macbeth is killed.

CRITICAL VIEWPOINT A02

When Macbeth hears of his wife's death his only thoughts are that she could have waited for a while. In Act I she was his dearest love and his 'dearest partner of greatness' (I.5.9–10). This suggests that the Witches' evil has blunted his senses, and his conscience has been seared.

ACT V SCENES 4 AND 5

SUMMARY

- The English and Scottish army meet at Birnam Wood.
- Malcolm orders his army to carry branches cut from the wood as camouflage and they march confidently towards Dunsinane.
- Macbeth learns of Lady Macbeth's death and hears that Birnam Wood is apparently physically moving towards Dunsinane.
- The Witches' promise, in which Macbeth put such trust, is revealed as open to different interpretations.

ANALYSIS

A SCENE OF CONTRASTS

The quiet confidence and the professionalism apparent in Malcolm's army are in sharp contrast to the shouting, boasting and disorganisation shown by Macbeth in the previous scene. All the Scottish nobles who have appeared earlier in the play are now allied against Macbeth. The contrast shows that Macbeth is doomed and upholds the view that the rightful king in waiting is going to be a good and just leader.

MACBETH'S DETACHMENT

It is possible that Macbeth's castle could withstand a long siege, but there is a mixture of boasting, detachment from ordinary life and loss in his claim that he is now unmoved by fear. Lady Macbeth's death, possibly by her own hand, reduces his bravado and resolution to empty words. Life seems futile and deceptive (compare his false words in II.3.88–93). The report of Birnan Wood's movement confirms the deceptiveness of the Witches' advice to Macbeth. He can now submit quietly or fight on, knowing the futility of his struggle, and he raises himself to fight. The future has no real meaning for him and, as his life stands, what lies ahead is a mere continuation of the present struggle, as captured in the effective repetition of 'Tomorrow and tomorrow and tomorrow' (5.19).

KEY QUOTATION: ACT V SCENE 5 A01

Key quotation: 'Life's but a walking shadow, a poor player / That struts and frets his hour upon the stage / And then is heard no more' (5.24–6).

- Macbeth is saying that life is nothing other than an illusion. Life is like a poor actor who struts and worries for his time on the stage and is gone.
- Shakespeare intends us to have sympathy with Macbeth at this point.
- Macbeth is feeling sorry for himself (or is depressed) and sees life as nothing more than 'a poor player'.
- Shakespeare is making a comment on life and Macbeth is a 'vehicle' for his comments.

GLOSSARY		
10	**Our ... before't**	us besieging it
11	**advantage to be given**	opportunity to escape presents itself
42	**pull in resolution**	check my confidence
47	**avouches**	alleges

ACT V SCENE 6

SUMMARY

- The English and Scottish army throw down their branches and Malcolm gives the order to start fighting.
- Macbeth kills Young Seyward but is then killed by Macduff.
- Malcolm is hailed as the new King of Scotland.

ANALYSIS

MACBETH'S DEATH

Shakespeare tries to convey on stage the action of the battle by having characters move on and off the central space, flitting before our eyes. The focus of our attention is, of course, Macbeth. He clings to the prophecy that he cannot be harmed by one born of a woman and accordingly fights with a curious nonchalance. Although his castle has fallen behind him, he fights on and seems to accept the inevitability of defeat only when the circumstances of Macduff's birth show again that the Witches told only a partial truth. He fights to the death rather than accept humiliation and we are moved by the helplessness of his final struggle. The play ends with the restoration of the order Macbeth had disrupted and a reassertion of the Christian values that Macbeth had overthrown.

KEY QUOTATION: ACT V SCENE 6 — A01

Key quotation: The Witches are described by Macbeth as 'juggling fiends' (line 58).

- Macbeth is saying here that the Witches are meddling evil creatures.
- Could this be linked back to the previous scene, where Macbeth sees them in league with 'the fiend'?
- Is this the point in the play where Macbeth knows he has been tricked, or has he realised before this moment?

GLOSSARY

4	**we**	the royal we
10	**clamorous harbingers**	noisy announcers
11	**stake**	pole (to which the bear was tied)
12	**bear-like**	baiting a tied bear with dogs was a popular sport
32	**bruited**	announced
40	**play ... fool**	commit suicide (honourable death for a defeated Roman general)
48	**intrenchant**	unable to be cut
51	**charmèd**	protected by magic
55	**Untimely ripped**	abnormally delivered
58	**juggling**	cheating

CONTEXT — A04

Old Seyward is an experienced soldier and he is mostly concerned that his son had 'his hurts before' (line 85) the battle – he is relieved to discover that they were 'on the front' (line 86). Seyward refuses to mourn for his son, as he did God's duty. This type of patriotism appears unfeeling to the modern reader, but would be acceptable to the Jacobean audience of the time.

CRITICAL VIEWPOINT — A01

Children are often treated violently in *Macbeth*. Lady Macbeth tells her husband that she would have 'dashed the brains out' of her child had she acted as Macbeth had done (I.7.58). In Act Four Scene 2, Lady Macduff's son is brutally murdered. Earlier in the play, Duncan's sons need to flee or their lives – as does Banquo's son. It could be argued, either that this brutalisation of children reflects contemporary life, or that it is a reflection of Macbeth's brutal regime.

CHARACTERS

MACBETH

WHO IS MACBETH?

- Macbeth begins the play as a soldier and Thane of Glamis.
- He is given the title Thane of Cawdor as a reward for his loyalty to Duncan, but following the Witches' prophecy he murders Duncan and takes his crown.
- He hires assassins to kill Banquo and Macduff's wife and children.
- He is killed by Macduff in a hand to hand fight.

MACBETH: A 'PEERLESS KINSMAN'?

In the reports of Macbeth's courage in battle, in the second scene of the play, he is 'brave Macbeth' and 'valour's minion' (I.2.16 and I.2.19). Duncan, acknowledging his champion, calls him 'valiant cousin' and 'noble Macbeth' (I.2.24 and I.2.70). In Act I there is only one reservation expressed about Macbeth's character, and in different circumstances it could be considered a compliment. This 'peerless kinsman' to King Duncan (I.4.59) is judged by his wife to have a nature 'too full o'the milk of human-kindness' (I.5.15) to allow him to kill Duncan. She recognises his ambition to be 'great' but feels that he would prefer to be given the throne by someone else, whatever methods were used, rather than grab it himself.

The second part of her analysis (I.7.47–53) points to a basic dishonesty in Macbeth and it is this aspect of his character that she ruthlessly attacks, hoping to overcome his doubts. His qualms and repulsion, before and after Duncan's murder, are denounced as cowardice and foolishness by his wife; and later, in Act III, she feels he has not improved.

CHECK THE BOOK **A03**

Read the account of Macbeth in Shakespeare's source, Holinshed's *Chronicles of England, Scotland and Ireland* (first published in 1587, and reprinted in an expanded edition in 1587), in order to evaluate exactly how much of Shakespeare's character is his own creation, and how much is 'historical'. Many texts of the play include the relevant passages from this source, but it is also available online.

STUDY FOCUS: UNSOLDIERLY BEHAVIOUR **A01**

Macbeth is a soldier in armour at his first appearance in the play and at his final exit. In between, we witness some very unsoldierly behaviour when he is frequently out of rational control. He is described as 'rapt' and 'brain-sickly' earlier on, 'sick at heart' and 'cowed' towards the end. In situation after situation he is preoccupied with speculations rather than facts. His awareness of this tendency leads him to observe:

Strange things I have in head, that will to hand;
Which must be acted ere they may be scanned. (III.4.138–9)

This comes at the end of the supper scene where he has undergone excruciating tortures in his mind at the appearance of Banquo's ghost. He can act only when he does not allow himself to think and, as a result, his actions become more frenzied as the play continues. Only in Duncan's murder does he participate directly and here he acts under pressure from his wife.

MACBETH AS A TYRANT

At the end of Act II, Macduff appears to anticipate Banquo's suspicions that he 'playedst most foully' to gain the throne. By the end of Act III the decline in Macbeth's reputation is obvious; his title of the second half of the play, 'tyrant', has been introduced (III.6.22). From now on there is not a good word uttered about Macbeth. Macduff claims that:

Not in the legions
Of horrid hell can come a devil more damned
In evils to top Macbeth (IV.3.55–7)

At the end of the play, the 'cursèd head' of the 'dead butcher' is displayed (V.6.94 and 108), leaving no doubt of Macbeth's terrible decline.

SUPERNATURAL ISOLATION

After Duncan's and Banquo's murders come the scenes where Macbeth's horror and conscience force themselves into his conscious mind to the neglect of everything else. In the case of the murder of Macduff's family, we do not see Macbeth again for over four hundred lines after he says, 'To crown my thoughts with acts, be it thought and done' (IV.1.148). The terrifying callousness of the crime seems beyond Macbeth's own comprehension. Each murder he commits, or commissions, is expected by him to end the 'restless ecstasy' he suffers but even before Duncan's murder he sees something of the futility of such an effort when he realises:

> that we but teach
> Bloody instructions, which, being taught, return
> To plague the inventor. (I.7.8–10)

Macbeth lays bare his thoughts in **asides** throughout the play and his confusion is apparent from very early on: 'This supernatural soliciting / Cannot be ill, cannot be good (I.3.129–30) and 'That function is smothered in surmise / And nothing is but what is not' (I.3.140–1). The Witches' prophecy appears clear and yet asks more questions than it answers, while the supernatural element causes Macbeth further concern.

We are presented with a man motivated to kill Duncan only because of ambition but who, having yielded to this desire, steps so far into blood that there is no turning back. As the play progresses, we are made aware of his peculiar isolation – as all escape routes are blocked off. Before Banquo's murder, Macbeth tells only a certain amount of his plans to his wife, who had been his 'dearest partner of greatness' (I.5.9–10), and without her his reliance on the Witches becomes greater. He recognises in Act V Scene 3 that:

> that which should accompany old age,
> As honour, love, obedience, troops of friends,
> I must not look to have. (lines 24–6)

AN INTOXICATING VILLAIN

Macbeth associates himself with darkness and evil and he has to be seen as a villain. How is it, then, that we retain an interest in Macbeth and may even feel some sympathy for him? The answer must lie in the weight of evidence about him presented from the inside. We hear from his own heart of his ambition, his weakness – the wrongness of his behaviour and his deceits. We are made aware of the intoxication he feels at his own evil. Macbeth, as a man, is weak and he finds a misplaced strength in his viciousness. In his dialogue we notice a shift from a diplomatic, hollow ornateness to a blustering, bullying language full of exclamations, questions and commands. However, these are all equally hollow. In the final act, Macbeth concedes to himself that his strutting and fretting are empty gestures but, chained as he is like a bear, he will not surrender. We cannot but admire his affirmation that he 'will try the last' (V.6.71).

KEY QUOTATION: MACBETH **A01**

Key quotation: 'Life's but ... a tale / Told by an idiot, full of sound and fury, / Signifying nothing' (V.5.24–8).

- Macbeth is saying that life is like a story told by a fool. Life is full of noise and disturbance but devoid of meaning.
- In the Christian world of the play, this is a shocking expression of nihilism and atheism.
- To a modern audience, Macbeth's despair is seen by some as no more than the poetic expression of how humans are insignificant.

CRITICAL VIEWPOINT **A03**

The Ancient Greeks' idea of a tragic hero was someone who was a hero but had a character flaw which brought about his destruction. Tragic heroes were commonly born of noble birth and, therefore, their descent evoked more pity. Macbeth qualifies as a tragic hero (under the Greek definition) and some commentators have seen ambition as his fateful character flaw. Other commentators believe that Macbeth has very few redeeming features, however, and does not qualify as a tragic hero in the same way that Othello and Hamlet do.

LADY MACBETH

WHO IS LADY MACBETH?

- Lady Macbeth is Macbeth's wife and the mistress of Dunsinane Castle.
- She persuades Macbeth to murder King Duncan.
- Initially full of self-will and discipline, she is eventually overcome by her conscience.

LADY MACBETH'S AMBITION

Shakespeare offers no background to explain Macbeth's ambition to be king. There is a similar abruptness in the nature of Lady Macbeth as she appears in Act I Scene 5. When she reads of the Witches' prophecy in Macbeth's letter, there is no indication of doubt, suspicion or hesitation in her reaction. Her one worry concerns Macbeth's ability to fulfil or enact the prophecy and she is confident that the 'valour of my tongue' will persuade him (I.5.25). By the time Macbeth arrives, several minutes later, she has mobilised her whole being towards the task of Duncan's murder. She is prepared to sacrifice her femininity and her humanity to 'Give solely sovereign sway and masterdom' to Macbeth and herself (I.5.68).

ABSOLUTE PURPOSE

In all the public scenes in the play, Lady Macbeth acts 'like the innocent flower'; in the private scenes we see the 'serpent under't' (I.5.63–4). She is full of purpose and discipline – her control of the situation is immaculate. We identify with Macbeth and are morally paralysed by her power of will. In Act I Scene 7, we see Macbeth's feeble questions and attempts to draw back. These are smashed aside by her counter questions and a mixture of taunting and practicality – forcing Macbeth into sharing her resolution. In the scene of the murder there is a contrast between the narration of Macbeth and the sharp rebukes and practical detail of his wife. Macbeth is stuck in his own imagination but she refuses to see anything other than immediate actions. We should not be surprised, however, as she has evoked evil spirits to fill her 'from the crown to the toe top-full / Of direst cruelty' (I.5.40–1).

DOUBTS CREEP IN

Lady Macbeth manages to maintain this same control over herself during the supper scene with Banquo's ghost. However, earlier, in Act III Scene 2, we have heard her first private thought since the murder of Duncan:

> Naught's had, all's spent,
> Where our desire is got without content.
> 'Tis safer to be that which we destroy
> Than by destruction dwell in doubtful joy. (lines 4–7)

Macbeth enters at this point and she changes her attitude immediately – attempting to eradicate in Macbeth the uncertainty we know she feels in herself. It is noticeable in this scene that after her initial words of comfort, she is allowed no time to speak by Macbeth and, for the first time, we hear her say 'What's to be done?' (III.2.44). She does not know of Macbeth's plans for Banquo, and planning has passed from her hands to Macbeth.

CHECK THE BOOK **A03**

A. C. Bradley's *Shakespearean Tragedy* (1904) presents a coherent and detailed approach to Shakespeare's plays through the study of their characters. Writing about Lady Macbeth, he remarks that in the opening act she is 'the most commanding and perhaps the most awe-inspiring figure that Shakespeare drew'.

STUDY FOCUS: LADY MACBETH'S POWERS SLIP **A02**

After the supper scene, when the guests have departed, Macbeth shows his leadership. The power in the relationship has shifted back to Macbeth. Lady Macbeth appears only once more, in her sleepwalking scene at the beginning of Act V. This sleepwalking scene is very important to the play structurally because it summarises the murders commissioned by Macbeth and takes place before Malcolm's assault. The questions that intrigue readers are:

- Why has Lady Macbeth changed since Act I?

- What has happened to the rigid self-discipline?

The answer seems to lie in that very rigidity. Macbeth, who started from a weaker position, has had some release in his own imaginings and he has come to terms with his deeds. He has gradually come to accept his precarious stance. His wife has only once in our hearing suggested that her contentment is incomplete. Gradually, Lady Macbeth's repressed conscience and her knowledge that the 'sovereign sway and masterdom' have not materialised have forced themselves into her dreams. At this point, as the Doctor says, she re-enacts the murders in her sleep. The contrast between her curt assurance in Act II Scene 2 and her vulnerability in Act V Scene 1 is painfully ironic. Her possible suicide is the final desperate act of the mind seeking to cleanse itself. Perhaps the evil spirits she evoked in Act I, having served their purpose, have left her. The once strong queen is now weak and vulnerable.

GRADE BOOSTER **A01**

It might be helpful to note down all you know about Lady Macbeth up until the banqueting scene, then note down all you know about her when she reappears in Act V, until her death. You can check for yourself how she has changed.

KEY QUOTATION: LADY MACBETH **A01**

Key quotation:

''Tis safer to be that which we destroy
Than by destruction dwell in doubtful joy.' (III.2.6–7)

- Lady Macbeth is saying that it is better to be the person who is murdered than to be the killer and plagued by anxiety.

- Lady Macbeth has got all that she has wanted but has no peace of mind.

- Having killed Duncan, the Macbeths are tormented by guilt and find no security in their elevated position. These two lines allow us into the mind of Lady Macbeth – we know what she really thinks and are prepared for her death in Act V.

BANQUO

WHO IS BANQUO?

- A brave and loyal soldier in Duncan's army, and an ancestor of James I.
- He is friend of Macbeth – until they meet the Witches: Banquo is murdered by hired assassins because of Macbeth's jealousy.
- He finally appears as a ghost, with a role to rebuke Macbeth.

BANQUO'S VIRTUES

For the first half of the play, Banquo is very obviously presented by Shakespeare as a parallel figure to Macbeth. Both distinguish themselves by fighting for their king, both have promises made to them by the Witches; but there the similarity ends. In Act I Scene 4, Banquo's reply to the king's praise is brief and self-effacing – Macbeth's is fuller. From our knowledge of Macbeth's thoughts in the previous scene, we suspect it is dishonest. In contrast, Banquo's brevity can be equated with truthfulness and honour.

BANQUO AND THE WITCHES

In Act I Scene 3, Banquo's reaction to the Witches is noticeably more casual than Macbeth's, although he does ask the Witches if they see anything in the future for him. In their equivocal replies they promise him greatness and happiness, in comparison with Macbeth. In the play Banquo appears morally superior to Macbeth and we could argue that he is never unhappy in the tortured manner of his friend. The Witches' significant prediction, however, is that his descendants will become kings. Both men are genuinely startled at the immediate fulfilment of the prediction that Macbeth will become Thane of Cawdor. Banquo's puzzlement takes the form of scepticism and a deep distrust of the Witches, whom he sees as the 'devil' or the 'instruments of darkness' (I.3.106 and 123). This distrust later becomes fear when, in Act II Scene 1, he tells of the 'cursèd thoughts that nature / Gives way to in repose' (lines 8–9) and we find out in line 20 that he has been dreaming of the Witches. Unlike Macbeth, he prays for God's help ('Merciful powers', II.1.7) against whatever 'cursèd thoughts' he has dreamed up.

CRITICAL VIEWPOINT A01

It is Macbeth who tells us about Banquo's 'royalty of nature' (III.1.49), and it is he who praises Banquo's excellence (I.7.16–20). Why does Shakespeare use Macbeth to tell us about the goodness of Banquo's character and what does this tell us about Macbeth?

MACBETH'S JEALOUSY OF BANQUO

Macbeth is taunted by two aspects of Banquo, as he explains in Act III Scene 1 lines 48–71. The first, the virtue and strength of character of Banquo, is a rebuke to Macbeth's weaker character. The second is more subjective: it would appear that Macbeth cannot tolerate the thought that he has sacrificed his soul to profit Banquo, by allowing the latter's descendants to become kings. These two aspects remain to torment Macbeth's mind after the murder of Banquo and the escape of Fleance, and we can argue that Banquo's ghost arrives when summoned by Macbeth's conscience. At the point when Macbeth tries to dismiss Banquo with words, the ghost comes to rebuke him. Macbeth's impotent rage at the survival of Banquo's line in the Witches' show of eight kings in Act IV Scene 1 expresses itself in the massacre of Macduff's 'wife, his babes, and all unfortunate souls / That trace him in his line' (IV.1.151–2).

STUDY FOCUS: BANQUO'S MOTIVATION   A04

To please James I, Shakespeare portrays the king's ancestor Banquo as a good Christian. But is there anything hidden in the text? We are left puzzling why Banquo fails to share his suspicion that his friend 'playedst most foully' (III.1.3) for the kingship. Banquo fails to mention the meeting he and Macbeth had with the Witches. Is this because he was told his sons would become kings?

KEY QUOTATION: BANQUO A01

Key quotation: Banquo, at the end of his soliloquy, says 'But hush! no more' (III.1.10).

- Banquo is saying to himself to be quiet and to say nothing else.
- Banquo is succumbing to the Witches but overcomes his temptations by ending his soliloquy.
- Banquo knows someone is coming, so he stops thinking aloud.
- Banquo takes the Witches' prophecies seriously and makes a decision to keep his thoughts about Macbeth to himself.

THE WITCHES

WHO ARE THE WITCHES?

- The Witches are portrayed as instruments of evil and do not appear as solid creatures.
- They seek to lead Macbeth to harm Scotland and bring about his destruction.

THE WITCHES' PURPOSE

The Witches' purpose is at first unclear, but their connection with Macbeth is signalled right from the start. Macbeth is peculiarly vulnerable to their influence because they voice the desires of his own heart. After his initial fear of being caught out (I.3.50–1), his mind moves easily along the route they indicate towards the 'imperial theme' (I.3.128). The Witches' nature is continually evoked and invoked in speeches by Macbeth and Lady Macbeth and their very sexlessness (I.3.44–6) seems to correspond with Lady Macbeth's prayer against her own nature in Act I Scene 5 lines 38–52.

In Act IV, Macbeth is able to find the Witches when he chooses but he wants to hear only what favours himself. Too late he comes to realise that the Witches have their own purposes which are not for man's benefit. The equivocation theme, which is central to the play, operates most obviously through the Witches – they are the most striking voices of unnaturalness and disorder. Lady Macbeth offers no comment on the Witches, the 'metaphysical aid' (I.5.27), who promise so much to her husband. It is Macbeth who needs the Witches to tell him what is in his own mind and what he is afraid to acknowledge as his own. The Witches, of course, do not make promises; they utter riddles which Macbeth in his weakness interprets in his own apparent interest. He is, therefore, not deceived by the Witches but by his ill-founded reliance on his own interpretation.

CHECK THE FILM A03

Examine several film versions of *Macbeth* to see how successful the directors are in their attempts to make the Witches convincingly frightening. On stage they present even greater difficulties for a modern audience.

KEY QUOTATION: THE WITCHES A01

Key quotation:

He shall spurn fate, scorn death, and bear
His hopes 'bove wisdom, grace, and fear.
And you all know security
Is mortals' chiefest enemy. (III.5.30–3)

- Hecat is saying that Macbeth will be fooled into thinking he is greater than fate and he will mock death. He will consider himself above wisdom, grace and fear. Overconfidence is man's greatest enemy.
- This suggests that Macbeth has no control over his own destiny.
- Hecat realises that Macbeth only operates for himself.
- Hecat is showing the other witches that she's in charge.

MACDUFF

WHO IS MACDUFF?

- Macduff is the Thane of Fife – he is loyal to Duncan and upset by his death.
- He is willing to defy Macbeth by refusing to attend the coronation and banquet, and puts his family at risk by meeting Malcolm in England.
- He is the soldier who kills Macbeth.

MACDUFF'S HONESTY

With his knocking at the gate, Macduff's entrance marks the first intrusion of the outside world on Macbeth's murder of Duncan. Through the remainder of the play, he continues to annoy and challenge Macbeth. In Act II Scene 4 lines 37–8, he voices the first suspicion of Macbeth when Macduff, having decided not to attend Macbeth's coronation, suggests that the new regime may not be a comfortable one. He keeps clear of Macbeth's 'solemn supper' and at the end of the supper scene Macbeth's plans of further murders appears to include the uncooperative Macduff.

THE MURDER OF MACDUFF'S FAMILY

Shakespeare's handling of the scene in Macduff's castle emphasises the family affection and the vulnerability of Lady Macduff and her son – who are left defenceless by the absence of Macduff. Macduff's act of political bravery, in effect, sacrifices his innocent family to the brutality of tyranny. His bravery and honesty emerge in the long scene with Malcolm and in the end it is a poetic justice that Macduff should be the one to execute Macbeth. The final confrontation brings from Macbeth his only public confession of guilt when he says in Act V Scene 6 'my soul is too much charged / With blood of thine already' (lines 44–5).

CRITICAL VIEWPOINT A03

Macduff's remark, 'He has no children' (IV.3.215), in the painful scene when he tries to come to terms with the murder of his entire family, is generally taken to refer to Macbeth. This suggests either that such a deed could only be committed by a man who has no offspring of his own, or that no exact revenge can be possible to requite his loss. But it is ambiguous, and may also refer to Malcolm's attempts to console him. Sigmund Freud in his essay on *Macbeth* examines the implications of Macduff's outburst.

STUDY FOCUS: MACDUFF VS MACBETH   A02

The humanity of Macduff's reaction to the news of his family's killing – 'But I must feel it as a man' (IV.3.220) – is in complete contrast to the inhumanity of the perpetrator, Macbeth, and this controls the conclusion of the play. We see the torment and the emptiness of Macbeth's life and we turn in relief to the dignity and humanity of Macduff and the order re-established by Malcolm. Macbeth, the usurper and overreacher against those values, is exposed as a 'dwarfish thief' in a 'giant's robe' (V.2 21–2). The contrast between Macbeth and Macduff cannot be greater.

KEY QUOTATION: MACDUFF   A01

Key quotation: 'Macduff was from his mother's womb / Untimely ripped' (V.6.54–5).

- Macduff explains to Macbeth that he was technically not born of woman, thus making it obvious to Macbeth that he has lost and should give up the will to fight.
- Shakespeare makes it clear that Macbeth should not have trusted the Witches.

DUNCAN

WHO IS DUNCAN?

- Duncan is a dignified, gentle and appreciative king.
- He is too trusting of the wrong people.
- He is murdered by Macbeth.

AVOIDING DUNCAN

Duncan is murdered by Macbeth in Act II Scene 2, but in the eight scenes before that he has met Macbeth only once. Macbeth himself seems to avoid the king as much as possible so that it is Lady Macbeth who welcomes Duncan to Inverness. It is interesting that Macbeth does not even remain in the supper room with the king. Macbeth is aware of Duncan's virtues and sees the enormity of his proposed murder of him.

Act I Scene 6 offers a picture of peace and trust in complete contrast to Scene 5 and the second half of Scene 7. Even Lady Macbeth sees a likeness to her own father in Duncan's sleeping face. Macbeth cannot think deeply about the intended murder and his hand seems to do a deed independently of his troubled mind. The treachery and deceit of Macbeth and Lady Macbeth are apparent in the ways they avoid calling the murder by its name but speak of 'business', 'provided for', 'deed'. Macbeth's theatrical description of Duncan in Act II Scene 3 lines 108–13 seems ornate and evades the horror. The reality of the murder is most fully felt in Lady Macbeth's chilling question much later: 'Yet who would have thought the old man to have had so much blood in him?' (V.1.38–9).

STUDY FOCUS: A MAN OF FAULTLESS VIRTUE? · A02

When Macbeth contemplates killing the king, he hesitates because 'Duncan has borne his faculties so meek' (I.7.17) and has been 'So clear in his great office' (line 18). Macbeth undoubtedly sees Duncan as a good king. Duncan's meekness is further emphasised by Macduff when he tells Malcolm 'Thy royal father / Was a most sainted king.' (IV.3.108–9). However, Duncan does not appear to be a good judge of character. He trusts the rebellious Thane of Cawdor and then begins to trust Macbeth. We also need to question why there is a rebellion against his rule, which almost crushes his kingdom. We can argue that Shakespeare's characters are rarely one-dimensional. They often display complex traits and flaws that make them all the more human and believable.

KEY QUOTATION: DUNCAN · A01

Key quotation: 'He was a gentleman in whom I built / An absolute trust' (I.4.14–15).

- Duncan is saying that he had complete trust in the Thane of Cawdor.
- This is a warning to the audience that Macbeth, the new Thane of Cawdor, will also rebel against Duncan's rule.
- Shakespeare is pointing out that Duncan is a poor judge of character.
- Duncan is making the point that you cannot be sure of a person's character no matter how secure you feel.

REVISION FOCUS: TASK 4 · A03

How far do you agree with the statements below?

- The murder of Duncan brought Macbeth great success.
- Macbeth immediately failed to find his kingship satisfying.

Try writing opening paragraphs for essays based on the discussion points above.

GRADE BOOSTER A02

Sometimes you need to look for clues in the text to ascertain details about characters. Duncan's exact age is not made clear, but he has two grown sons, which suggests he is not a young man. He does not physically fight for his kingdom, but awaits reports of the battle from other people and Lady Macbeth's awful utterance that she wouldn't have thought the old man would have so much blood in him again suggests that he is not young.

MALCOLM

WHO IS MALCOLM?

- Malcolm is King Duncan's son and is pronounced next in line to the throne.
- Along with his younger brother Donalbain he is accused of his father's murder.
- He assembles an army to defeat Macbeth and is proclaimed king at the end of the play.

MALCOLM'S FLIGHT

The flight of Malcolm after the murder of his father seems very sudden from the evidence given in the play. He is the chosen heir but he seems immediately to suspect that the fate of his father may come to him as well. In the early part of the play he is a dutiful attendant to his father. He appears to be a virtuous young man and is very gracious concerning the execution of Cawdor. He was probably wise to flee to England after his father's death as Macbeth had already identified his existence as a barrier to his ambitions.

THE LATER MALCOLM

When we next meet Malcolm at King Edward's court in Act IV Scene 3, it is evident that some time has elapsed since his flight from Macbeth's castle. Malcolm appears much more self-assured and he is well established at the English court.

In his meeting with Macduff, he reveals himself as a shrewd politician unwilling to commit himself until the evidence is clear. He tests Macduff's honesty, at the same time as presenting himself as the very opposite of Macbeth. In the final act he is the instrument by which good government is to be restored to Scotland (with the help of England) and his deference to law and order is apparent not only in his final speech but also in the scenes leading up to the battle – he is willing to bow to the knowledge of more experienced men. The connection between his style of speaking in his final speech and his father's manner in Act I Scene 4 demonstrates the reassertion of virtue in the person of the king.

> **CHECK THE FILM** A03
>
> The portrayal of Malcolm in Roman Polanski's *Macbeth* as sly and evil-looking has no justification in Shakespeare's text.

ROSS

WHO IS ROSS?

- Ross tells Duncan of Macbeth's victories and discusses the strange day after Duncan's murder.
- He is with Lady Macduff before she is murdered.

LOYALTY

Ross is loyal to Duncan and, later, loyal to Malcolm. He first appears in Act I Scene 2 as he praises Macbeth as 'Bellona's bridegroom' (line 56) and informs Duncan that the Norwegian king 'craves composition' (line 62).

DUPLICITY

The character of Ross can be questioned. Is he politically expedient? When he speaks to Macduff concerning the death of Duncan, both men choose their words carefully. They both have their doubts that the guards accepted bribes from Duncan's sons and murdered the king. However, Ross sees Macbeth crowned at Scone while Macduff stays away. Later on, Ross visits and warns but does not try to save Lady Macduff.

> **CRITICAL VIEWPOINT** A03
>
> What do we know about Ross? Check the times he appears in the play and check what others say about him. Is he an astute politician and is he loyal to any one person?

THEMES

AMBITION

VAULTING AMBITION

Macbeth and Lady Macbeth are both extremely ambitious and their ambition contributes directly to the tragedy of the play. Lady Macbeth initially views her husband as ambitious 'but without / The illness should attend it' (I.5.17–18). In other words, Macbeth is a brave warrior who wants to succeed but who does not want to get his hands dirty by committing evil deeds. However, he is driven by his ambition to seek power, and with the prompting of the Witches and his wife commits the acts he at first shied away from. Although he immediately regrets the killing of Duncan – 'wake Duncan with thy knocking. I wouldst thou couldst' (II.2.74) – Macbeth still retains his ambition. From this point onwards he is focused on finding ways to keep his hold on the throne.

RETAINING POWER

When Macbeth has the crown, he wishes to keep it within his family – even though the evidence suggests he has no children. This desire to pass the crown on to a future family member leads him to believe he can defy the Witches' prophecy for Banquo. This self-belief impels him to hire assassins to murder Banquo and his son, Fleance. The fact that Fleance escapes brings Macbeth to the realisation that not all his ambitions will be met. He then focuses his ambition on retaining power for himself.

As Macbeth plots each murder, he believes he will find the solution to his objective – that of making his position safe. Each murder, he judges, will be his last. The murder of Banquo is designed to destroy the man whose genius is superior to Macbeth's own. The murder of Macduff's family suggests a tyrant's ambition to hold on to power at whatever cost.

> **CRITICAL VIEWPOINT A03**
>
> Banquo fails to tell other nobles about the meeting with the Witches and keeps his own council concerning his suspicions that to become king, Macbeth 'playedst most foully for't.' (III.1.3). This could lead us to the conclusion that he is less than honest when it comes to ambition for his children.

> **CRITICAL VIEWPOINT A03**
>
> One of Banquo's key roles is to show Macbeth that there are moral choices and he clearly indicates to Macbeth that he intends to keep his 'bosom franchised, and allegiance clear' (II.1.28).

STUDY FOCUS: LADY MACBETH'S AMBITION A02

Lady Macbeth's ambition appears unchecked and she is the driving force behind the murder of Duncan. She pursues her ambition with a great determination. She willingly seeks evil to aid her in her objective and asks evil to fill her 'from the crown to the top-full / Of direst cruelty' (I.5.40–1). She asks that no feelings of womanly humanity will upset her ruthless intention of making sure that her husband becomes king – and she becomes queen. The fact that evil spirits have now entered her body allows her to almost force her husband to kill Duncan. The same self-determination, driven by ambition, helps her to keep strong just after the murder of Duncan. At this point, she is Macbeth's crutch, holding him up and urging him on.

For the remainder of the play, she is passive in watching Macbeth commit more atrocities while she is driven into madness and despair. It is their tragic fate that both Macbeth and his wife regret the fruit of their unbridled ambition.

KEY QUOTATIONS: AMBITION A01

Key quotation: '"Hail king that shall be!" This have I thought good to deliver thee, my dearest partner of greatness' (I.5.9–10).

- Macbeth is saying 'Hail to the future king! I wanted to share this news with you, my dearest partner in greatness.'
- Macbeth, at this point shares everything with his wife. He wants to tell her the news concerning the Witches – and his thoughts – as soon as he possibly can.
- Shakespeare wants his audience to immediately know Lady Macbeth's character. Her reaction to the letter allows us to be aware of her ambition.

GUILT

A GUILTY CONSCIENCE?

Macbeth is essentially a play concerning how the protagonists are tormented by guilt that eventually leads to their destruction. Before he murders Duncan, Macbeth feels guilt at the thought of becoming king. The Witches' prophecies startle him (Act I Scene 3). Even at this early stage, Macbeth shows his surprise – which implies a guilty conscience. Does this suggest he possibly contemplated becoming king before the Witches met with him on the heath? Banquo noted his reaction and asked 'Good sir, why do you start' (I.3.50).

AFTER THE REGICIDE

In Act II Scene 2, having murdered Duncan, Macbeth looks upon his blood-stained hands. He can only utter 'This is a sorry sight' (line 20). He is already guilty – knowing that the only reason for killing the king who was 'so meek' and 'so clear in his great office' (I.7.17 and 18) was 'vaulting ambition' (I.7.27). He felt guilty before the murder because he knew that while Duncan was staying at his castle 'in double trust' (I.7.12) he should have 'against his murderer shut the door' (I.7.12). He was also Duncan's near relative and the king's subject. He defended Duncan in the battlefield and should have defended the king in his castle. Macbeth felt guilty before he entered the king's chamber and it could be suggested that the blood-covered daggers that led Macbeth to the chamber are the very manifestations of his guilt. When he believes he cannot 'wash this blood / Clean from my hand' (lines 60–1), the implication is that he can never wash away his guilt because regicide is so terrible a crime.

LADY MACBETH'S GUILT

Lady Macbeth, at this point, feels that 'A little water clears us of the deed' (line 67). But in Act V Scene 1, when sleepwalking, she mimics rubbing her hands and declares 'who would have thought the old man to have had / so much blood in him' (lines 38–9). She is unable to free herself of the guilt of murdering a king and it is likely that she feels responsible for the murder of Banquo and for the butchering of Macduff's family. She relentlessly bullied Macbeth into the regicide and knows she is to blame for the consequences that stemmed from the murder.

FINAL RELEASE?

Macbeth's tortures continue after his paid assassins murder Banquo. The ghost that appears at the banquet is only seen by Macbeth and is, most likely, the product of his guilt. Finally, before Macbeth fights Macduff in hand to hand combat, he declares 'My soul is too charged / With blood of thine already' (V.6.44–5). Although Macbeth's heart appears seared by the time we reach Act V, deep within him he carries the guilt for the murder of Macduff's innocent wife and children. Modern critics might imply that only death, at the hand of Macduff, releases Macbeth from the guilt that makes him re-evaluate life. However, the Jacobean audience would have believed that Macbeth would face eternal damnation for his deeds. He cannot 'jump the life to come' (I.7.7).

KEY QUOTATION: GUILT **A01**

Key quotation: 'Of all men else I have avoided thee' (V.6.43).

- Macbeth is saying that Macduff is the only one that he has avoided.
- Macbeth wanted to avoid Macduff due to the Witches' warning.
- Macbeth is feeling guilty – as he hired the assassins to murder Macduff's wife and children.

CONTEXT **A04**

When Shakespeare wrote *Macbeth* the Gunpowder Plot (1605) was still fresh in people's minds. There had also been assassination attempts upon the life of James I, meaning that the theme of guilt – linked to the crime of regicide – would have been politically acceptable to the king.

CRITICAL VIEWPOINT **A03**

Having murdered Duncan, Macbeth believes he will never sleep peacefully again. Sleep is seen as a prerogative of those who have no guilty conscience. It is evident that Macbeth does not sleep and when he does he is plagued by nightmares. In contrast, the good Duncan is murdered while sleeping the deep sleep of the just.

KINGSHIP

DUNCAN AS KING

Shakespeare thoroughly explores the theme of kingship in *Macbeth*. The first king we meet is Duncan. He is always referred to as the king, whereas Macbeth is soon known as the tyrant. Macbeth, when contemplating the murder of Duncan, is aware of the kingly qualities he possesses. He notes that Duncan's 'virtues / Will plead like angels' (I.7.18–19). This view of Duncan is reinforced by Macduff when he declares to Malcolm that Duncan 'Was a most sainted king' (IV.3.109). We know Duncan was a good man but was he a good king? It would appear that he had one character flaw that may have led to the rebellion and certainly led to his death – his lack of ability to understand people's motives and his trust of the wrong people. Of the treacherous Thane of Cawdor, Duncan states 'He was a gentleman on whom I built / An absolute trust' (I.4.14–15). He transfers the title to Macbeth, who is driven by 'vaulting ambition' (I.7.27) and misreads Macbeth's castle as a place that 'hath a pleasant seat' (I.6.1). It will soon be the place of his death. Lady Macbeth fools him into calling her 'Fair and noble hostess' (I.6.24). Arguably this inability to judge character leads, ultimately, to his death.

BANQUO'S KINGLY QUALITIES

Banquo is a loyal subject of the king. After the battle, he receives no reward other than a hug from the king. Duncan recognises Banquo has 'no less deserved' (I.4.31) honours. From the evidence in the play, it is likely that Banquo would have made a good king. Macbeth recognises his qualities when he jealously acknowledges Banquo's courage and wisdom, declaring that his own 'genius is rebuked' (III.1.55).

> **CONTEXT** A04
>
> James I was patron of Shakespeare's company The King's Men, so it was expedient for Shakespeare to write a play dealing with the issues that James would approve.

STUDY FOCUS: MALCOLM AND MACBETH — A02

A key discussion of kingship takes place between Malcolm and Macduff in Act IV Scene 3. In testing Macduff, Malcolm lists all the characteristics of a tyrant. These are voluptuousness (sexual pleasure), avarice and a lack of kingly graces. By pretending that these are his personal faults, Malcolm points out that these are the marks of a tyrant – and by implication Macbeth's. Malcolm lists the graces that he tricks Macduff into thinking he does not possess. They are 'justice, verity, temp'rance, stableness / Bounty, perseverance, mercy, lowliness / Devotion, patience, courage, fortitude' (lines 92–4). We are aware that Malcolm knows what is expected from a king and can be confident that when he rules Scotland, healing will take place through his kingship. Crucially, he does not possess his father's gullibility; he is aware that Macbeth tried to entice him back to Scotland. He is also politically shrewd in testing that Macduff was not sent by Macbeth to lure him to his death.

Macbeth, in contrast, is portrayed as a tyrant. Despite his bravery in battle, which initially inspires trust and loyalty, he does not possess kingly qualities and is viewed as a man thirsty for power, violent and of an impulsive temperament. Macbeth can only bring chaos which shows itself in the form of freak weather and supernatural events. He also brings death and destruction, offers no justice and is instrumental in the murdering of innocents. For us, he becomes the embodiment of tyranny. Scotland can only be healed when Macbeth is killed.

KEY QUOTATION: KINGSHIP — A01

Key quotation: 'If thou couldst, doctor, cast / The water of my land, find her disease, / And purge it to a sound and pristine health' (V.3.50–2).

- Macbeth is saying, can you work out what's wrong with my country? Can you diagnose its disease and bring it back to health?
- Macbeth is referring to the English invasion of his country – which he appears to imply is like a disease.
- Shakespeare uses irony to suggest that Scotland would be better off without Macbeth.

THE SUPERNATURAL

THE WITCHES

We discover in Act I Scene 3 that the Witches possess certain supernatural powers. They are able to control the elements, 'And the very ports they blow' (line 15). Banquo's description of the Witches shows us that they are not human and not gender specific. He comments; 'You should be women / And yet your beards forbid me to interpret / That you are so' (lines 44–6). The Witches have powers to predict both Macbeth's and Banquo's futures and the truth of these predictions is borne out during the play. Shakespeare makes sure we understand that the Witches are real and not a figment of Macbeth's imagination by allowing both Macbeth and Banquo to see and to talk with them. Yet, the Witches vanish and Banquo asks if he and Macbeth have 'eaten the insane root / That takes the reason prisoner?' (lines 83–4). Much later, they lead Macbeth to believe he is invincible and only at the last does he realise 'these juggling fiends' have tricked him (V.6.58). Their role seems to be to give Macbeth a reason for killing Duncan – so their predictions can be fulfilled. They trick Macbeth into believing he can do as he wishes, thus encouraging his moral descent. It is clear that Shakespeare wants us to know they are evil.

STUDY FOCUS: THE APPARITIONS A04

The three apparitions would have thrilled the Jacobean audience. The armed head, a bloody child and a child crowned with a tree in his hand (IV.1) would all evoke a sense of horror in the minds of the audience – who really would have believed in such occurrences. The grotesque ingredients thrown in the cauldron and the potion that is conjured up would certainly be seen as the literal products of evil. Of course, they are exciting images of Gothic horror and would look frighteningly effective on stage.

THE SUPERNATURAL AND NATURE

After the murder of Duncan there are supernatural occurrences within nature, to show us that the natural order has been disturbed. Lady Macbeth claimed that she heard 'The owl-scream and the cricket's cry' (II.2.15). It is as if nature's creatures are aware that something terrible has occurred. Just before the discovery of the murder, Lennox talks to Macbeth concerning the unruly night. He mentions that 'Lamenting heard i' th'air, strange screams of death' (II.3.53) and that the earth 'Was feverous and did shake' (line 58). The earth, in some supernatural way, has reacted to the death of the rightful king. In the following scene (II.4), Ross and an Old Man discuss the unnatural events outside the castle, which correspond to the unnatural occurrences inside the castle – Macbeth (owl) murdering Duncan (falcon). That the murder and the supernatural events occur at night creates a sense of fear and mystery and heightens suspense.

BANQUO'S GHOST

The ghost of Banquo creates further suspense and excitement. We could view it as an illusion – a product of Macbeth's mind. However, we do not know, until the scene ends, how this situation will turn out for Macbeth. Will he reveal that he has hired assassins to murder Banquo?

KEY QUOTATION: THE SUPERNATURAL A01

Key quotation: Hecat speaks angrily to the three witches: 'all you have done / Hath been for a wayward son' (III.5.10–11).

- Hecat is saying that the Witches have worked for a man who acts like a spoiled child.

- Hecat is telling the Witches that they have helped someone who is not empathetic to their cause. She is aware that Macbeth's sole motivation is ambition.

PART FOUR: STRUCTURE, FORM AND LANGUAGE

STRUCTURE

By the 'structure' of a play we mean how the whole play is made up of its parts and how these parts relate to each other. A play is not a gallery of portraits (the characters), nor is it a series of incidents (the plot), although both of these elements are very important. Even in a play as rich in incident as *Macbeth*, we learn most about the meaning (impact) of a play through the dialogue. For example, when Duncan talks about Macbeth's castle, he says 'This castle hath a pleasant seat' (I.6.1). However, we are aware that Macbeth and Lady Macbeth are planning to murder him while Duncan is ignorant of the threat to his life and views the castle as a pleasant place. The contrast between language and setting, combined with character and the order of events, creates a potent mix here, ripe for analysis.

A SHORT, FAST-PACED PLAY

Macbeth is the third shortest play written by Shakespeare and one of the immediately striking aspects of it is the speed at which the action occurs. Although *Macbeth* is only two-thirds the length of *King Lear*, it is divided into the same number of scenes; the scenes are very brief compared with the scenes in *King Lear* – and their brevity increases a sense of frenetic movement. The military action in Act I, for example, is condensed in order to demonstrate Macbeth's heroism. Always, throughout the play, the focus of our attention is fixed firmly on Macbeth. For example, in Act I Scene 5, Macbeth does not appear until after line 50, but it is his letter that Lady Macbeth reads, it is his character that she analyses. In Act IV Scene 3, where we have a long discussion between Macduff and Malcolm on the subjects of loyalty and good kings, Macbeth is never out of our minds. We know what he has done to Macduff's family, we can see that the invented portrait Malcolm offers of himself is really a description of Macbeth and we hear the contrast between the 'good king' (Edward) and the evil Macbeth.

However distant from each they may be in actual geographical terms, in the play Fife, Forres, Inverness, Scone, Dunsinane and Glamis are all brought within one day's riding time of each other. We know the state of Scotland and the kingship of Scotland is suffering under Macbeth's leadership – we also feel that the whole natural world is participating in this suffering. This perception enlarges the struggle in the play until it not only involves a whole country but also beyond Scotland to that of the soul of mankind. No sooner do the Witches voice a prophecy than it is fulfilled; no sooner does Macbeth inform his wife of the Witches' prophecy, and she considers the possibilities, than the Messenger arrives with the news that the king is coming to spend the night. In the final act the stretch of time from Lady Macbeth's sleepwalking to Macbeth's death seems to last only as long as it takes us to read the pages. This compression of time heightens our excitement and sense of suspense.

CINEMATIC VIEWPOINTS

Unlike many of Shakespeare's plays, *Macbeth* has no subplot, or secondary action. The play concentrates on Macbeth. How is it, then, that the play offers so much more than the analysis of one man? One reason for this lies in the way Shakespeare juxtaposes what, in cinematic terms, would be called close-up shots and longer-range shots. Shakespeare uses the lesser characters to comment on the central action, to give a wider context to Macbeth's behaviour. Each act, with the exception of Act I, ends with such a scene where we are helped to take stock of the situation. For example, in Act III Scene 6, Lennox and the unnamed Lord are not in themselves important to the play but they act as a pressure gauge to measure the tyranny of Macbeth and to register the wider significance of Macbeth's evil. The scenes with Duncan and later with Malcolm are presented as examples of decent kingly order against which Macbeth is to be judged. Equally, the scenes with the Witches show an abyss of anti-human evil on the edge of which mankind stumbles and into which Macbeth enters.

CHECK THE BOOK A03

For ideas about order and disorder in Shakespeare's plays, a good starting point is E. M. W. Tillyard's *The Elizabethan World Picture* (1943). The absolute significance Shakespeare gives to 'degree' (a person's importance due to their rank) may be questioned; but see the discussion of Ulysses' speech from *Troilus and Cressida* on this subject in Chapter 2, where the picture of the chaos that results from 'degree' being shaken is reminiscent of Macbeth's Scotland after the murder of Duncan.

CHECK THE BOOK A03

It is interesting to check the use of settings in *Macbeth*. Events happen on open heathland, inside and outside castles. The stories in *The Bloody Chamber* (1995) by Angela Carter are often set in wild places – such as a castle, a ruined stately home (described as a Palladian House), the Beast's ruined palace and wild woods. The landscapes in *Macbeth* are often desolate and wild (the heath) and much of the action takes place in the dark. This is also true of the *Bloody Chamber* collection. Bleak landscapes are also a feature of Mary Shelley's *Frankenstein*.

FORM

It is important that you are able to discuss the form of the play to fulfil AO2.

THE HISTORY GENRE

CHECK THE BOOK **A03**

Compare Macbeth's suitability as a king with the suitability as a husband of the Marquis from *The Bloody Chamber* by Angela Carter.

In the 1590s Shakespeare wrote nine plays dealing with England's dynastic history. These history plays cover a large span of time and examine a wide diversity of incident and experience. Although it is a serious oversimplification to see these plays as crude propaganda for the legitimacy of Elizabeth's position as queen, it is an undeniable truth that they were written at a very special time and appealed to patriotic, Protestant Englishmen in a particular way. Richard III, who seized the throne and held it by cruelty and deception, was a cautionary example of a bad king. The young, irresponsible Henry became King Henry V. On ascending the throne, he found qualities in himself which made him a popular and heroic king. Many of Shakespeare's plays examine situations of political ambitions and power. The setting may be Rome, Denmark, fifteenth-century England or eleventh-century Scotland. Never before had a dramatist journeyed (in his imagination) so widely for his material – but the repeated investigation indicates the contemporary fascination with political order and disorder.

GRADE BOOSTER **A02**

The form of a literary work means its shape and structure – and its style. Form also means the type of work the piece is – for example, short story, poem or essay. In this case, the form is a play, and within that contains aspects of the genres of history and tragedy.

STUDY FOCUS: MACBETH AS A HISTORY PLAY **A04**

For *Macbeth*, Shakespeare used the same source as he had used for the English history plays, Raphael Holinshed's *Chronicles of England, Scotland and Ireland*, first published in 1577, and reprinted in 1587. Shakespeare never followed Holinshed slavishly but created plays based on material he found in the *Chronicles*. We can learn much about Shakespeare's dramatic intentions from the difference between his *Macbeth* and that portrayed by Holinshed. The characters are differentiated and developed in a manner completely unlike the original; Duncan is made into a good king and Macbeth into an almost totally brutal one; Banquo, the ancestor of King James, becomes an honest man whereas in Holinshed he helps Macbeth to murder Duncan; greater prominence is given to the Witches; and the sense of time and location is more tightly organised to suggest a concentration of action.

THE TRAGEDY GENRE

CRITICAL VIEWPOINT **A03**

In his controversial study of the play, *Witches and Jesuits: Shakespeare's Macbeth* (1995), Garry Wills suggests that the play can only be understood in relation to the Gunpowder Plot of 1605 and the surrounding political events.

The Greek writer Aristotle provides the earliest surviving literary explanation for tragedy. He defined the genre as characterised by seriousness and dignity. Tragedy involved a great person who experienced a reversal of fortunes. The reversal of fortune was usually downward – and should bring about pity and fear for the audience. The structure of the best tragedy should be complex and the reversal of fortune must be caused by the tragic hero's **hamartia** (mistake) – which we often interpret as a character flaw. The reversal of fortune, according to Aristotle, is inevitable and irreversible. By the end of the play, the protagonist should have learned something about fate, destiny or his own failings.

MACBETH'S CHARACTER FLAW

Macbeth fits into this category because, although he is a brave soldier, his reversal of fortune is due to the almost insatiable ambition that he and Lady Macbeth share. It brings about their destruction. Shakespeare makes it clear that Macbeth is unsuited to the new roles he obtains during the play. His clothing **imagery** illustrates this. Macbeth feels he is 'dressed in borrowed robes' (I.3.108) and when he becomes Thane of Cawdor, Banquo states that 'New honours come upon him / Like our strange garments, cleave not to their mould' (I.3.144–5). Towards the end of the play, as Macbeth's powers slip from him, Angus comments that the title of Kingship 'Hang loose about him, like a giant's robe / Upon a dwarfish thief' (V.2.21–2).

THE GOTHIC

THE HISTORY OF GOTHIC NOVELS

Horace Walpole's *The Castle of Otranto* (1764) is often regarded as the first **Gothic** novel. Walpole was obsessed with medieval Gothic architecture and built his own house in that style. He used elements of the Gothic style for the settings in his novel, which was popular and sold well. Although, by modern standards, it might be considered dull, it was a hit in 1764 and other writers penned their own Gothic novels. This type of novel became a recognisable genre and the features of such novels are used in modern horror films.

THE FEATURES OF A GOTHIC NOVEL

A Gothic novel is generally understood to require some or all of the following features:

- a castle – often ruined or haunted
- dungeons and/or underground passages and crypts
- labyrinths or dark corridors and winding staircases
- bleak landscapes – such as mountains, icy wastes, extreme weather, thick forests
- horrific murders
- conspiracies
- 'doubling' and disguise
- the supernatural – including supernatural manifestations
- magic and omens or ancestral curses
- an anti-hero driven by passion or an evil villain
- terrifying events or the hint of such events
- a cross-over between life and death
- confusion, chaos and disorder.

Many elements of the Gothic genre are recognised in classic novels such as *Jane Eyre* and *Wuthering Heights*. In *Wuthering Heights* we have love crossing over the boundaries between life and death. The setting in *Wuthering Heights* is a bleak moor and the main building is dilapidated and foreboding. Lockwood, one of the narrators, has a dream in which Catherine appears as a ghost. We suspect her ghost is not the figment of Lockwood's imagination when Heathcliff flings open the window and begs Catherine's ghost to enter.

THE GOTHIC IN *MACBETH*

Although *Macbeth* predates the Gothic horror genre, Shakespeare uses many features of the Gothic. His settings are in and around various castles and some of the scenes are in darkness or in poor light. The conspiracy to murder Duncan is talked about in a room of the castle – away from other people. The heath, where Macbeth meets the witches, is a bleak landscape and can be compared to the landscape around *Wuthering Heights*.

The extreme weather, such as thunder and lightning whenever the witches appear, or the wild weather after the murder of Duncan, can be compared to the weather described in *Frankenstein* and *Wuthering Heights*. The horrific murders of Duncan, Banquo and Macduff's family can be compared to the murders in *Frankenstein*. The supernatural elements in *Macbeth* are the Witches, the dagger and Banquo's ghost, and there are further Gothic features in the movement of the forest, the anti-hero driven by ambition, the terrifying events and the fear of further atrocities. In *Macbeth* magic and omens are used in the form of the Witches' prophecies and the conjuring of the three apparitions. If *Macbeth* is not primarily seen as a Gothic play, there are strong features of the Gothic within it.

CHECK THE BOOK A03

It is good to be aware of other plays that have some similarities with *Macbeth*. *The White Devil* is a revenge tragedy that explores the differences between the way people depict themselves and what they are really like. *The Changeling* involves murders and intrigue. Beatrice has her betrothed murdered by the man who loves her.

CHECK THE BOOK A03

In *The Bloody Chamber*, the Marquis appears to be haunted by a family curse.

CRITICAL VIEWPOINT A02

In Mary Shelley's *Frankenstein*, Frankenstein, like Macbeth, is tortured by guilt and jealousy and it is the guilt and jealousy that drives the monster to act by destroying others. Frankenstein inadvertently destroys most of his family by his ambition. The bleak settings in remote places featuring in the novel *Frankenstein* add to its Gothic elements.

LANGUAGE

IMAGERY

In a good play the dramatist seeks to make the ideas, characters and developments vivid and memorable. One way of achieving this aim is to associate, for example, a character with certain qualities or activities. When these occur in the play, the audience remembers the character and comes to a fuller understanding of him or her. In Shakespeare's later plays, particularly, **imagery** is a very important element. It gives the texture of the play's density and richness. Some images, of course, are striking individually, but it is more rewarding to see the imagery as functioning in strands which help to connect, reinforce and enliven the shifts in the play as a whole. The richness of Shakespeare's imagery must inevitably suffer in translation and some is certainly lost in modern English.

The idea of contrasts lies at the heart of *Macbeth* and this is the focus for the section below. Other strands which could be explored are those concerned with the themes of deceit, unnaturalness, killings, innocence and obligation.

CHECK THE BOOK A03

Two respected twentieth-century studies of Shakespeare's imagery are Caroline Spurgeon's *Shakespeare's Imagery and What It Tells Us* (1935) and Wolfgang Clemen's *The Development of Shakespeare's Imagery* (1951).

ORDER AND HEALTH VERSUS DISORDER AND SICKNESS

In Act I Scene 4 we have a scene of royal order when Duncan, pleased with his success in the battle, distributes justice and rewards. Great emphasis is placed on the ties that bind a subject to his king and mutual trust is ceremoniously communicated. At the end of the scene, Duncan says (of Macbeth):

And in his commendations I am fed;
It is a banquet to me. Let's after him
Whose care is gone before to bid us welcome.
It is a peerless kinsman. (I.4.56–9)

Gradually through the play, we come to recognise 'banquets' as an image of order. After the supper in Macbeth's castle, Duncan is described by Banquo as having been 'in unusual pleasure' (II.1.13) and he is now 'In measureless content' (II.1.17). In Act III Scene 1, Macbeth issues a special invitation to Banquo to 'a solemn supper' (line 14), and when the supper begins in Scene 4, the new king is careful about the formal arrangements and the guests sit according to their 'degrees' (III.4.1). An intimation of disorder comes in the form of the Murderer with blood on his face, hardly a suitable guest, and when Macbeth rebukes the absent Banquo, he brings disorder to the table. The supper is broken up by Lady Macbeth's command:

Stand not upon the order of your going;
But go at once. (III.4.118–19)

When the lords leave the table they do not leave by degrees. The important guests and those lower in rank leave together – showing disorder.

Furthermore, the unnamed Lord in Act III Scene 6 prays that:

           we may again
Give to our tables meat, sleep to our nights,
Free from our feasts and banquets bloody knives,
Do faithful homage and receive free honours. (lines 33–6)

In Act IV Scene 3, Malcolm enumerates the virtues of kingship (lines 92–4) and King Edward is obviously presented as an example of a good king whose personal qualities are matched by his ability to make his people healthy by divine healing from God. It is from this court of good order that Malcolm sets out to bring back 'wholesome days' to Scotland, and the discipline and dedication evident in his army are in contrast to the poor morale in Dunsinane Castle.

STUDY FOCUS: IMAGES OF DISORDER AND SICKNESS

Throughout the play there occur images of disorder and sickness. From the 'hurly-burly' of the first scene, through the 'revolt' and 'broil' of the battle, to the sense of hallucination with the Witches, we are presented with the disturbance of a calm. Drunkenness is important in the first two acts (see I.7.36, II.1.31, II.2.1–2 and the Porter scene in Act II Scene 3). In the second act, Macbeth comments on his 'heat-oppressèd brain' (II.1.39), and his wife accuses him of being 'brain-sickly' (II.2.46). In the opening scene of Act III, Macbeth tells the Murderers that '[We] wear our health but sickly in his [Banquo's] life' (III.1.106) and in the following scene his wife tries to comfort him, saying: 'Things without all remedy / Should be without regard' (III.2.11–12). His mind is 'full of scorpions' (III.2.36) and he is determined to bring ruin on the universe:

Ere we will eat our meal in fear, and sleep
In the affliction of these terrible dreams
That shake us nightly. (III.2.17–19)

Two scenes later, his lack of inner control becomes public in his 'solemn supper' when his vision of Banquo's ghost reduces him to a nervous wreck so that he breaks the 'good meeting' (III.4.108). Such symptoms continue throughout the remainder of the play and are shared by Lady Macbeth, whose repressed conscience gives way in her sleepwalking scene.

Macbeth's personal condition is reflected in the disorder in nature on the night of Duncan's murder (see Act II Scene 4) and subsequently in a sickness in the kingdom of Scotland described to Lady Macduff by Ross (IV.2.14–22) and to Malcolm by Macduff (IV.3.4–8). The Doctor, of whom Macbeth makes such impossible demands later, says in Act V Scene 1 'unnatural deeds / Do breed unnatural troubles' (lines 67–8) and his diagnosis describes accurately the situation where the personal disorder of the king who 'cannot buckle his distempered cause / Within the belt of rule' (V.2.15–16) is reflected in his country and in the world of nature.

LIGHT AND GRACE VERSUS DARKNESS AND EVIL

From the moral confusion suggested by the Witches' 'Fair is foul, and foul is fair' at the beginning (I.1.9), the play gradually moves to show the irreconcilable distinction between good and evil, and equates this with contrasting images of light and dark. When in Act I Scene 4, Duncan pronounces that 'signs of nobleness, like stars, shall shine / On all deservers' (lines 42–3), he is immediately challenged by Macbeth's private prayer:

Stars, hide your fires,
Let not light see my black and deep desires.
The eye wink at the hand; yet let that be
Which the eye fears, when it is done, to see. (I.4.51–4)

In Act I Scene 5 Lady Macbeth promises Macbeth that there shall be no sun for Duncan in the morning as a result of 'This night's great business' (line 66). Just before Macbeth enters, his wife, in words reminiscent of his in the previous scene, prays:

Come, thick night,
And pall thee in the dunnest smoke of hell,
That my keen knife see not the wound it makes,
Nor heaven peep through the blanket of the dark
To cry, 'Hold, hold!' (I.5.48–52)

CONTEXT A04

James I was a keen believer in the divine right of kings. The king was seen as God's ruler on earth, so the king represented the state. To murder the king would be to harm the country and go against God's will.

CONTEXT A04

Grace is used in its Christian sense of the helping power of God.

Macbeth is well aware of the sinfulness of his plan to murder Duncan and in his **soliloquy** in Act I Scene 7 he recognises the purity of Duncan, who is 'So clear in his great office' that 'his virtues / Will plead like angels' (lines 18–19) against Macbeth's use of the 'poisoned chalice' (line 11), an act of complete sacrilege.

It is easier to trace the two sets of **imagery** separately but it is of fundamental importance to appreciate that they comment on each other; light/grace and darkness/evil together emphasise the moral force of the play. In Macbeth's description of the murder of Duncan, the sons of the king pray for God's blessing, and in Macduff's Duncan is 'the Lord's anointed temple' (II.3.65). Banquo, who at the beginning of Act II asked for the help of the 'Merciful powers' against wicked thoughts (II.1.7), after the murder states: 'In the great hand of God I stand' (II.3.127).

In Act III Scene 6 we are told that Malcolm has been welcomed by 'the most pious Edward with such grace' (line 27) and the Scottish noblemen pray that a 'holy angel' will help to bring a 'swift blessing' on Scotland (III.6.45–7). Again, as in the case of the order–disorder imagery, Act IV Scene 3 is very important in emphasising the difference between foulness and grace. Malcolm's words in lines 18–24, the description of King Edward (noted for his piety) and Macduff's confession of his sinfulness in lines 220–7 all demonstrate that the forces against Macbeth trust in different, purer powers (lines 237–8) from his dark guides.

The contrary images of darkness and evil are particularly obvious in the Witches, shrewdly observed by Banquo in Act I Scene 3 to be 'the instruments of darkness' (line 123). We quickly find Macbeth invoking the foulest spirits and darkening his conscience with images of sorcery and evil. His words immediately before the murder indicate clearly why he cannot say 'Amen' during the murder. Banquo's suspicion in Act III Scene 1 that Macbeth had 'playedst most foully' to become king (line 3) revives echoes of the earlier instances of 'foul', and if he were to have overheard Macbeth committing himself to darkness (III.2.45–56) he would have understood just how foul Macbeth's mind has become. By Act III Scene 4, after the disruption of the supper, Macbeth is stuck between darkness and day.

IDENTIFICATION WITH EVIL

Macbeth's self-identification with evil seems complete when in Act IV Scene 1 he conjures the Witches to answer his enquiries; the 'secret, black, and midnight hags' (line 47) are the instruments of evil and unnaturalness. In Act V Scene 1, Lady Macbeth concedes in her dreams that 'Hell is murky!' (line 35); she who had invoked 'thick night' (I.5.48) now requires 'light by her continually' (lines 22–3). The Doctor declares the case needs divine care but Macbeth, obviously in a similar condition, is beyond repentance, and claims that he is beyond fear.

In the final scene of the play we find Shakespeare employing **Gothic** language to describe Macbeth as a 'devil' (V.6.18), 'hellhound' (line 42), a follower of Satan (line 53) and a 'rarer monster' (line 64). Macbeth has killed Young Seyward, a soldier of God, according to his father, who sees the war against Macbeth as a holy war against evil.

The two strands of imagery of order and grace are completed in the final lines of the play which mark the defeat of disorder and evil.

VERSE AND STYLE

Macbeth is, for the most part, written in **blank verse**. The basic unit of blank verse is a line in **iambic pentameter** without a rhyme scheme but, increasingly in his plays, Shakespeare's use of the line and the number of its syllables and stresses became freer. A strict iambic pentameter has ten syllables with the stress falling on the even ones, for example: 'And wákes it nów to loók so gréen and pále' (I.7.37). Shakespeare's verse is seldom as regular as this but the pattern is there below the changing surface – resulting in regularity with flexibility. The sense and the punctuation do not stop dead at the end of lines. They often cross into the following line, giving a feeling of the unevenness of spoken English.

By grouping stressed syllables, Shakespeare catches the emphasis and intensity of a character, for example: 'Whiles night's black agents to their preys do rouse' (III.2.53), where Macbeth's grim fascination with nastiness is brought out by the voice stress on 'night's black agents'. Occasionally, Shakespeare uses rhyming couplets. A considerable number of scenes intimate their conclusion by this means but there are two other significant uses of rhyme. The witches commonly speak in rhyme, often using a shorter line and a different stress pattern – to give a sound of incantations and charms. More interesting is the fact that Macbeth uses rhyming couplets more often than any other character and more than the heroes of Shakespeare's other tragedies. It does seem that Macbeth has an affinity with the Witches.

STUDY FOCUS: SHAKESPEARE'S USE OF PROSE　A02

Prose in Shakespeare's plays often denotes the low social rank of a character, or it occurs in a situation which is abnormal, in some way, to the ordinary behaviour of the play. In *Macbeth* there are four situations where prose is used: Macbeth's letter to his wife, Act I Scene 5; the Porter scene, Act II Scene 3; the conversation between Lady Macduff and her son, Act IV Scene 2; and the sleepwalking scene, Act V Scene 1. The letter has to be written in prose, but what have the other three scenes in common? They all present characters who seem artless or in a state of mind where verse would appear contrived. The Porter can ramble on in his rude, somewhat incoherent way because of the amount of alcohol he has drunk. The mother and her child, talking of birds and traitors and fathers, soften from the formality of verse to informal prose – which is easier on the ear. They revert to the more formal verse when strangers enter! In her sleepwalking, Lady Macbeth loses the customary controls of verse and talks 'straight' for the first time in the play. Lady Macbeth's attendants, lower in the social scale, can talk in verse only when she has departed.

CONTEXT　A02

Blank verse is the commonest metre in English verse, and the normal medium of Elizabethan and Jacobean drama. It is also the form used in most of the greatest narrative works in English literature, such as John Milton's *Paradise Lost* (1667), William Wordsworth's *The Prelude* (1850) and Alfred Tennyson's *Idylls of the King* (1842–85).

GRADE BOOSTER　A03

It's important to keep in mind that Shakespeare's characters do not voice his opinions; they speak out of their dramatic situation. That is, to understand fully a speech or an exchange of dialogue, it is necessary to hear the words in their context in the play. It is impossible to deduce what Shakespeare's attitude to life was from reading Macbeth's speech in Act V Scene 5 beginning 'Tomorrow, and tomorrow, and tomorrow' (lines 19–28). This speech does not suggest Shakespeare is tired of life, but is a powerful evocation of Macbeth weary state of mind at the end of the play.

CHECK THE BOOK　A03

Two different kinds of reference books about Shakespeare's language are *A Shakespeare Glossary* by C. T. Onions (1911, frequently reprinted); and Eric Partridge's *Shakespeare's Bawdy* (revised edition, 1955).

CONTEXT **A04**

Machiavelli wrote *The Prince* in 1532. It was a political book that appeared to approve a certain type of political behaviour. His critics claim that he advised political leaders on how to tyrannise their subjects. He also appeared to accept immoral and criminal acts and disregard the needs of individuals.

HISTORICAL CONTEXT

SHAKESPEARE'S AGE

Shakespeare arrived in London just as the rejuvenating movement in European culture (which since the nineteenth century has been known by the term 'Renaissance') was gaining momentum. Meaning literally 'rebirth', it denotes a revival and redirection of artistic and intellectual endeavour which began in Italy in the fourteenth century in the poetry of Petrarch. It spread gradually northwards across Europe, and is first detectable in England in the early sixteenth century in the writings of the scholar and statesman Sir Thomas More and in the poetry of Sir Thomas Wyatt and Henry Howard, Earl of Surrey. Its keynote was a curiosity in thought which challenged old assumptions and traditions. To the innovative spirit of the Renaissance, the preceding ages appeared dull, unoriginal and conformist.

CHANGES THAT INFLUENCED SHAKESPEARE

The spirit of the Renaissance was fuelled by the rediscovery of many classical texts and the culture of Greece and Rome. This fostered a confidence in human reason and in human potential which, in every sphere, challenged old convictions. The discovery of America and its peoples (Christopher Columbus had sailed in 1492) demonstrated that the world was a larger and stranger place than had been thought. The cosmological speculation of Copernicus (later confirmed by Galileo) that the sun, not the earth, was the centre of our planetary system challenged the centuries-old belief that the earth and human beings were at the centre of the cosmos. The pragmatic political philosophy of Machiavelli seemed to cut politics free from its traditional link with morality by permitting to statesmen any means which secured the desired end. The religious movements we know collectively as the Reformation broke with the Church of Rome and set the individual conscience, not ecclesiastical authority, at the centre of the religious life. Nothing, it seemed, was beyond questioning, nothing impossible.

CHECK THE BOOK **A03**

Benedict Anderson's book on the rise of the nation and nationalism, *Imagined Communities* (revised edition, 1991), has been influential for its definition of the nation as 'an imagined political community' – imagined in part through cultural productions such as Shakespeare's plays that deal with history, such as *Macbeth*.

STUDY FOCUS: SHAKESPEARE, THE INNOVATIVE PLAYWRIGHT **A04**

Shakespeare's drama is innovative and challenging in exactly the way of the Renaissance. It questions the beliefs, assumptions and politics upon which Jacobean society was founded. And although the plays always conclude in a restoration of order and stability, many critics are inclined to argue that their imaginative energy goes into subverting, rather than reinforcing, traditional values. Convention, audience expectation and censorship all required the status quo to be endorsed by the plots' conclusions. However, the dramas find ways to allow alternative sentiments to be expressed. Frequently, figures of authority are undercut by some comic or parodic figure. The despairing, critical and disillusioned are represented repeatedly and heard in the plays, rejecting, resenting, defying the established order. They always belong to marginal, socially unacceptable figures, such as the Old Man, the Porter and the Witches. These figures are 'licensed' by their situations to say what would be unacceptable from socially privileged or responsible citizens. The question is: are such characters given these views to discredit them, or were they the only ones through whom a voice could be given to radical and dissident ideas? Is Shakespeare a conservative or a revolutionary?

SHAKESPEARE'S USE OF THE COURT

Shakespeare often portrays the world of the court and his dramatic gaze is not always admiring; through a variety of devices, a critical perspective is brought to bear. The court may be paralleled by a very different world, revealing uncomfortable similarities (for example, Henry's court and the Boar's Head tavern, ruled over by Falstaff in *Henry IV*). Its hypocrisy may be bitterly denounced (for example, in the outbursts of the mad King Lear) and its self-seeking ambition represented disturbingly in the figure of a Machiavellian villain (such as Edmund in *King Lear*) or a malcontent (such as Iago in *Othello*). Shakespeare is fond of displacing the court to another context, the better to examine its assumptions and pretensions and to offer alternatives to the courtly life (for example, in the pastoral setting of the Forest of Arden in *As You Like It* or Prospero's island in *The Tempest*). Courtiers are frequently figures of fun whose unmanly sophistication ('neat and trimly dressed, / Fresh as a bridegroom … perfumed like a milliner', says Hotspur of such a man in *Henry IV Part 1*, I.3.33–6) is contrasted with plain-speaking integrity: Oswald is set against Kent in *King Lear*. In *Macbeth*, Shakespeare can be seen as upholding the status quo but points out the flaws in the court. He illustrates the dangers of being a usurper but also allows Duncan to be seen as a weak king.

PROTESTANTISM

Henry VIII caused a scandal by breaking with Roman Catholicism in the 1530s and in Shakespeare's time, the Pope had excommunicated Henry's daughter Elizabeth I as a heretic. When James I came to the throne, Catholic plots and attempts on the king's life led to a deep distrust of Catholics as potential traitors. It was important for Shakespeare to show that he supported the king's views when he wrote *Macbeth*: the murder of the rightful king had to appear evil and the consequences of regicide had to be portrayed as catastrophic for that individual.

Shakespeare's plays are remarkably free from direct religious sentiment, but their emphases are Protestant. Young women, for example, are destined for marriage, not for convents (precisely what Isabella appears to escape at the end of *Measure for Measure*); friars are dubious characters, full of schemes and deceptions, if with benign intentions, as in *Much Ado About Nothing* or *Romeo and Juliet*.

The central figures of the plays are frequently individuals beset by temptation, by the lure of evil – Angelo in *Measure for Measure*, Othello, Lear, Macbeth – and not only in tragedies: Falstaff is described as 'that old white-bearded Satan' (*Henry IV, Part 1*, II.4.454). We follow their inner struggles. Shakespeare's heroes have the preoccupation with self and the introspective tendencies encouraged by Protestantism: his tragic heroes are haunted by their consciences, seeking their true selves, agonising over what course of action to take as they follow what can often be understood as a kind of spiritual progress towards heaven or hell.

CONTEXT **A04**

When thinking of these matters, we should remember that stage plays were subject to censorship, and any criticism had therefore to be muted or oblique: direct criticism of the monarch or contemporary English court would not be tolerated. This has something to do with why Shakespeare's plays are always set either in the past, or abroad.

CONTEXT **A04**

The 'Bare ruined choirs where late the sweet birds sang' in Shakespeare's Sonnet 73 is thought to allude to the ruins of the monasteries which were dissolved in 1536–9 by Elizabeth I's father, Henry VIII, after his break with Roman Catholicism.

SHAKESPEARE'S THEATRE

The theatre for which the plays were written was one of the most remarkable innovations of the Renaissance. There had been no theatres or acting companies during the medieval period. Performed on carts and in open spaces at Christian festivals, plays had been almost exclusively religious. Such professional actors as there were wandered the country putting on a variety of entertainments in the yards of inns, on makeshift stages in market squares, or anywhere else suitable. They did not perform full-length plays, but mimes, juggling and comedy acts. Such actors were regarded by officialdom and polite society as little better than vagabonds and layabouts.

Just before Shakespeare went to London all this began to change. A number of young men who had been to the universities of Oxford and Cambridge came to London in the 1580s and began to write plays which made use of what they had learned about the classical drama of ancient Greece and Rome. Plays such as John Lyly's *Alexander and Campaspe* (1584), Christopher Marlowe's *Tamburlaine the Great* (*c*.1587) and Thomas Kyd's *The Spanish Tragedy* (1588–9) were unlike anything that had been written in English before. They were full-length plays on secular subjects, taking their plots from history and legend, adopting many of the devices of classical drama, and offering a range of characterisation and situation hitherto not attempted in English drama. With the exception of Lyly's prose dramas, they were in the unrhymed **iambic** pentameters (**blank verse**) which the Earl of Surrey had introduced into English earlier in the sixteenth century. This was a freer and more expressive medium than the rhymed verse of medieval drama. It was the drama of these 'university wits' which Shakespeare challenged when he came to London.

A PROFESSIONAL THEATRE

The most significant change of all, however, was that these dramatists wrote for the professional theatre. In 1576 James Burbage built the first permanent theatre in England, in Shoreditch, just beyond London's northern boundary. It was called simply 'the Theatre'. Others soon followed. When Shakespeare came to London, there was flourishing drama, theatres and companies of actors waiting for him, such as there had never been before in England. His company performed at James Burbage's Theatre until 1596, and used the Swan and Curtain until they moved into their own new theatre, the Globe, in 1599. It burned down in 1613 when a cannon was fired during a performance of Shakespeare's *Henry VIII*.

The form of the Jacobean theatre derived from the inn yards and animal baiting rings in which actors had been accustomed to perform in the past. They were circular wooden buildings with a paved courtyard in the middle open to the sky. A rectangular stage jutted out into the middle of this yard. Some of the audience stood in the yard (or 'pit') to watch the play. They were thus on three sides of the stage, close up to it and on a level with it. These 'groundlings' paid only a penny to get in, but for wealthier spectators there were seats in three covered tiers or galleries between the inner and outer walls of the building, extending round most of the auditorium and overlooking the pit and the stage. Such a theatre could hold about three thousand spectators.

PLAYS FOR BLACKFRIARS

In 1608 Shakespeare's company, the King's Men, acquired the Blackfriars Theatre, a smaller, rectangular indoor theatre, holding about seven hundred people, with seats for all the members of the audience, facilities for elaborate stage effects and, because it was enclosed, artificial lighting. It has been suggested that the plays written for this 'private' theatre differed from those written for the Globe, since, as it cost more to go to a private theatre, the audience came from a higher social stratum and demanded the more elaborate and courtly entertainment which Shakespeare's romances provide. However, the King's Men continued to play in the Globe in the summer, using Blackfriars in the winter. Therefore, it is not certain that Shakespeare's last plays were written specifically for the Blackfriars Theatre, or first performed there.

CHECK THE BOOK A03

The most authoritative book on what we know about the theatre of Shakespeare's time is Andrew Gurr's *The Shakespearean Stage* (1992).

CONTEXT A04

Whereas now we would conceptualise a visit to the theatre as 'going to see a play', the most common Jacobean phrase was 'to go to hear a play' (as in *The Taming of the Shrew*, Induction 2.130) – thus registering the different priorities of the early modern theatre.

CONTEXT A04

Shakespeare's acting company would not have had personal copies of the script of the play. Instead they would only have been given their own lines to learn. This was to stop plagiarism.

LITERARY BACKGROUND

For AQA Unit Four, you will be required to compare *Macbeth* with two other texts of your choice. For EDEXCEL Unit Two, you will be required to compare *Macbeth* with a play from 1300 to 1800 and with another play of your choice. Below are some possible ideas. For AQA/B Unit 3, *Macbeth* is listed as a **Gothic** text – please refer to **Part Four: Form** and the section on **The Gothic**.

PLAYS BY SHAKESPEARE AND HIS CONTEMPORARIES

Julius Caesar by William Shakespeare shares some themes with *Macbeth* in that it involves supernatural predictions (Ides of March), the assassination of the rightful ruler, Caesar, the ghost of Caesar and the conspiracy to murder Caesar. The weather is violent before the murder and there are omens and portents on the night of the murder. Brutus claims Caesar had to die as he ruled Rome only for personal ambition, but when Caesar's will is read to the crowd by Anthony, the crowd realise the assassins themselves acted for reasons of personal ambition. As the play ends, order is restored and it transpires that, of the assassins, only Brutus acted for what he perceived to be the good of Rome. There are many comparisons between this play and *Macbeth*. There are possibilities to explore the use of the supernatural in both plays, the consequences of murdering the rightful ruler and the consequences of ambition.

The Spanish Tragedy by Thomas Kyd (written between 1582 and 1592) contains several murders, a vengeful ghost and injustice. The theme of madness is explored through the characters of Isabella and Hieronimo and there are two suicides – that of Isabella and Bel-Imperia. There is the possibility of exploring revenge in *Macbeth* (Macduff's driving force after the death of his wife and children) with revenge in *The Spanish Tragedy*. Madness is a further theme that can be explored through this play and *Macbeth* – perhaps linking it with Ophelia's madness in *Hamlet*.

Doctor Faustus by Christopher Marlowe (1604) is a play about ambition and overreaching. Faustus grows dissatisfied with the limits of his scholarly knowledge and rejects conventional knowledge for magic and the occult – which ultimately brings about his destruction. The play has comparisons with *Macbeth* in that both men are ambitious, both overreach and are ultimately destroyed. Macbeth is killed by Macduff and Faustus is dragged off to hell. Both men see the error of their ways – but too late.

CHECK THE BOOK A03

Faust by Johann Wolfgang von Goethe is from the same German legend as Marlowe's play and deals with the same issues, although there are significant differences between Goethe's and Marlowe's versions.

VICTORIAN NOVELS

Jane Eyre by Charlotte Brontë (1847) explores (amongst other issues) the themes of love and passion, atonement and forgiveness. Rochester is a Bluebeard-type character who locks his mad wife in the attic and keeps her from the public eye. Jane Eyre is a self-reliant early **feminist** who is both the weaker and, later, the stronger character in the relationship between her and Rochester. There are comparisons and contrasts between Macbeth and his wife in this novel in terms of the madness of Lady Macbeth, the presence of dark secrets and the balance of power in their marriage.

Great Expectations by Charles Dickens (1860) deals with unrequited love (Pip for Estella and Miss Havisham for Compeyson) but it also deals with madness. Miss Havisham's obsessive behaviour after she is jilted by Compeyson leads to her destruction. The events can be compared with the relationship between Lord and Lady Macbeth and with Lady Macbeth's madness, while *The Woman in White* by Wilkie Collins (1860) explores the theme of madness and love and can be linked to *Macbeth* and *Great Expectations*.

MODERN TEXTS

A modern novel to look at might be *Atonement* by Ian McEwan (2001), which explores the themes of love, betrayal and the burden of guilt. *Couples, Passerby* by Botho Strauss (1981) concerns couples searching for a meaning but who only find lowliness and despair. *Wittgenstein's Nephew* by Thomas Bernhard (1980) reflects the tragic life and death of a close friend. The novel explores insanity and isolation – a possible comparison with Lady Macbeth. *Baltasar and Blimunda* by José Saramango (1982) is a novel in the magic realism genre. It explores the relationship between a soldier and a woman with magical powers, but their relationship is doomed.

The Skriker by Caryl Churchill (1994) is a modern play exploring issues such as love and revenge. The play combines English folk tales with modern urban life. The Skriker is a shapeshifter and death portent. The comparable issues with *Macbeth* are love (the breakdown of Macbeth's relationship with his wife), revenge (Macduff and Banquo's ghost) and the supernatural.

Song for a Dark Queen, a play by Nigel Bryant (1984), depicts a powerful woman (Boudicca) who resisted Roman rule but was eventually destroyed by the efficiency of the soldiers of Imperial Rome. The destruction of a powerful woman can be linked with Lady Macbeth. The play is an interpretation of the novel by Rosemary Sutcliff.

CHECK THE FILM **A03**

In the 2007 film version of *Atonement*, the themes of guilt and responsibility are clearly dramatised, and heightened by the backdrop of the Second World War.

CRITICAL DEBATES

SEVENTEENTH AND EIGHTEENTH CENTURIES

It is commonly held that *Macbeth* was first performed in 1606, and it has been popular ever since. It is one of the few plays by Shakespeare for which we have an eyewitness account in the playwright's lifetime. Simon Forman wrote a rough summary of the play when he saw it performed in 1611. After the Restoration and the reopening of the theatres, Sir William Davenant redevised *Macbeth* to include song and dance routines for the Witches and he regularised, in his view, some of the language and the verse. It would have been this heavily revised version of the play that Samuel Pepys saw and described in his diary in 1667, and the many productions until late in the nineteenth century were based on substantial adaptations of the text as we know it.

Samuel Johnson in his edition of *The Plays of Shakespeare* (1765) gathered together notes on *Macbeth* written twenty years earlier, in which he concentrated on a moral reading of the play and how the Witches would have been seen in Shakespeare's time: 'The danger of ambition is well described; and I know not whether it may be said in defence of some parts which now seem improbable, that, in Shakespeare's time, it was necessary to warn credulity against vain and illusive predictions. The passions [of the audience] are directed to their true end. Lady Macbeth is merely detested; and though the courage of Macbeth preserves some esteem, yet every reader rejoices in his fall.' About the same time as Johnson and sometimes after consultation with him, David Garrick, the most famous actor of the eighteenth century, restored much of the text which had been altered by Davenant but also introduced some changes, for example the removal of the Porter's scene and the presentation on stage of the death of Macbeth. Up to the end of the eighteenth century, the emphasis in writings on Shakespeare was on moral questions and on characters as representative of types of people.

NINETEENTH CENTURY

In 1794 Walter Whiter published his *Specimen of a Commentary on Shakespeare*, in which he analyses the language and characters in terms of word association. By tracing the recurrence of images in a speech, he identifies patterns in the mentality of a character. This more psychological reading of the plays anticipates the subtle interpretations of the inner lives of characters as practised by Thomas De Quincey, Samuel Taylor Coleridge and William Hazlitt in the first half of the century. De Quincey's essay, 'On the Knocking at the Gate in *Macbeth*' (1823), is wonderfully acute on the details of one scene. Some of the best criticism was based on particular productions of the play and the acting of such famous figures as J. P. Kemble, Edmund Kean and Henry Irving as Macbeth, and Mrs Sarah Siddons and Ellen Terry as Lady Macbeth (see photo). A Scottish professor of law, C. J. Bell, wrote in 1809 a fascinating, very detailed description of Mrs Siddons, showing how every intonation, gesture and movement caught a nuance of Lady Macbeth's personality. The essence of nineteenth-century criticism of the play was in examining the mystery and contradictory nuances of the characters Macbeth and Lady Macbeth.

CONTEXT **A04**

The first printed mention of Shakespeare, in a pamphlet of 1592 called *Greene's Groatsworth of Wit*, is written in the spirit of rivalry. He is referred to as an 'upstart crow' who thinks he is 'as well able to bombast out a blank verse as the best of you' and 'is in his own conceit the only Shake-scene in a country'.

CHECK THE BOOK **A03**

The six-volume *Critical Heritage: Shakespeare* (edited by Brian Vickers, 1995) brings together critical writing about Shakespeare from 1623 to 1802.

TWENTIETH CENTURY AND BEYOND

PSYCHOANALYTIC CRITICISM

CHECK THE BOOK **A03**

For a critical examination of psychoanalytic approaches to Shakespeare, see *Shakespeare in Psychoanalysis* by Philip Armstrong (2001).

A play dealing with hidden desires, dark forces, guilt and repressed fears could not but appeal to some of the new psychological thinkers early in the century, and Sigmund Freud showed a considerable if hurried interest in *Macbeth*. The different toughness in the characters of Macbeth and Lady Macbeth fascinated him and he offers an interesting suggestion that the husband and wife are really aspects of one personality but dramatically presented as two people. Although various psychological theories help to shape most readings of the play, it is only later in the century that **psychoanalytical** concepts became more central in some criticism. Derek Russell Davies's essay 'Hurt Minds' included in John Russell Brown's *Focus on Macbeth* (1982) offers an interpretation of *Macbeth* following on from, but also arguing with, some of Freud's categories and comments.

FEMINIST CRITICISM

Some **feminist** critics have focused on issues of gender and what they see as male and female values in the play. As early as 1962, in her essay 'General Macbeth', Mary McCarthy offered a stimulating and entertaining examination of the marital relationship between Macbeth and his wife. Marilyn French, in her essay '*Macbeth* and Masculine Values', sees a struggle between male aggressive insensitive force and a softer, maternal quality which is crushed in the play. In her book *Suffocating Mothers: Fantasies of Maternal Origin in Shakespeare's plays, Hamlet to The Tempest* (1992), Janet Adelman argues that the play is concerned with eliminating the female and trying to establish the male as self-sufficient. The Witches, in her reading, are allied to Lady Macbeth but both are disposed of by Macbeth.

OTHER VIEWS

CHECK THE BOOK **A03**

Marilyn French's '*Macbeth* and Masculine Values' examines notions of gender and manhood in the play in the *New Casebook Macbeth* (edited by Alan Sinfield, 1992). There is also a useful list of further reading on pages 98–100, including a section on gender and psychoanalysis.

Published in 1904 but still relevant, is *Shakespearean Tragedy* by A. C. Bradley. Bradley's study was massively influential for the first half of the twentieth century and remains very readable and rewarding today. He analyses the main characters as if they were actual people, and feels that we cannot laugh during the Porter's bawdy speech, as the moments either side of that scene are too momentous. Keith Thomas in *Religion and the Decline of Magic* (1973) discusses how Shakespeare's contemporaries thought about ghosts and witchcraft.

HISTORICIST CRITICISM

Seeing the play in such cultural terms has an obvious connection with **historicist** approaches. Of Shakespeare's tragedies, *Macbeth* is the most firmly rooted in the context of its original production, and some of its concerns can be seen as a continuation of Shakespeare's debate of political issues in the history plays (see **Form: The history genre**). This point is made by E. M. W. Tillyard in his *Shakespeare's History Plays* (1944). Henry N. Paul in *The Royal Play of Macbeth: When, Why and How It Was Written by Shakespeare* (1950) locates the play in considerable detail in its contemporary setting and in King James's interests and problems. Relevant passages from Holinshed's *Chronicles* are included in the Signet edition (1963) and the Arden edition (1970), and the reader is able to see how Shakespeare has used one of his major sources and to ask why. Terence Hawkes offers some suggestive lines of enquiry in relating the play to such events as the accession of James to the throne of a united Scotland and England, the Gunpowder Plot, and the colonisation of Ireland and New England. He also relates the play to ideas about witchcraft and national unity. Some of these contexts are explored in more detail in essays by Michael Hawkins, Peter Stallybrass, Steven Mullaney and Alan Sinfield in the 1980s and 1990s. These more recent essays can be described as **New Historicist** in that they demonstrate an awareness of how we read the past, of what we look for and give priority to in such a play – not just how the play fits with events of its own time.

CLOSE READING

In the 1930s, Caroline Spurgeon in England and Wolfgang Clemen in Germany independently developed a way of reading a Shakespeare play by tracing patterns of recurring **imagery**. In *Macbeth*, images of such elements as clothes, darkness, sickness and blood provided keys of interpretation for the reader or spectator. This focus on details of language fitted with the fashion of New Criticism prevalent from the 1930s to the 1960s. L. C. Knights in a famous essay 'How Many Children Had Lady Macbeth?' (1933, reprinted in his *Explorations*, 1946), argued vehemently against character-study or contextual readings: 'The only profitable approach to Shakespeare is a consideration of his plays as dramatic poems, of his use of language to obtain a total complex emotional response. Yet the bulk of Shakespearean criticism is concerned with his characters, his heroines, his love of Nature or his "philosophy" – with everything, in short, except with the words on the page, which is the main business of the critic to examine.' Cleanth Brooks offers a classic example of this method in his essay on *Macbeth*, 'The Naked Child and the Cloke of Manliness'. In her essay 'A Reply to Cleanth Brooks', Helen Gardner exposes a narrowness and artificiality in detailed explication of words and her doubts are taken up by some **postmodernist** critics such as Catherine Belsey in her essay 'Subjectivity and the Soliloquy', and Malcolm Evans in his 'Imperfect Speakers: the Tale Thickens' where the assumptions of close reading are seriously questioned.

RECENT CRITICS

Robert Shaughnessy's collection of essays *Shakespeare in Performance* (2000) examines the debates between theory and practice that have transformed our understanding of Shakespeare performance in the last decade. Drawing upon textual theory, cultural criticism, feminism and psychoanalysis, the essays address Shakespeare's plays as texts in and for performance in a variety of contexts, from the Renaissance to the present. Majorie B. Garber's *Shakespeare After All* (2004) is very readable and offers a complete and comprehensive introduction to Shakespeare's life and times. *Shakespeare's Unruly Women* by Georgiana Zegler (1997) is an interesting interpretation of how Shakespeare's female characters are crushed by the hierarchical male-dominated social structure of the times.

TARGETIN

It is very important to unde
cases, it is not enough simp
explore them in depth, dra

TYPICAL C GR

FEATU

 A01
You use critical vocal
your arguments mak
and focus on the tas
knowledge of the te

A02
You can say how so
form, structure and
meanings.

A03
You consider in det
between texts and
of texts differ, with
supporting referen

A04
You can write abou
factors and make s
links between thes

TYPICAL FEA

FEA

 A01
You use appropria
a technically fluen
are well structure
relevant, with a ve

A02
You explore and a
form, structure ar
perceptively how

 A03
You show a detail
understanding o
connections bet
consider differer
sharp evaluation
weaknesses. You
supportive refere

 A04
You show deep,
understanding
link to the text

PART SIX:

ASSESSME

WHAT ARE YO

The questions or tasks yo
AO1 to **AO4**.

You may get more mark
working on. Check with

WHAT DO TH

ASSESSME

AO1 Articulate creative
responses to litera
terminology and a
accurate written e

AO2 Demonstrate deta
analysing the way
language shape r

AO3 Explore connectio
different literary t
interpretations of

AO4 Demonstrate und
and influence of
texts are written

WHAT DOES

Depending on the cou

• Respond to a ge

**Explore the dram
elements in Macbe**

• Write about an a
studying. These
which you are i

**'Gothic literature
codes.' Discuss.**

• Focus on the pa
and others. For

**Compare and co
text(s) you have**

EXAMINER'S

Make sure you kn
set. This can help
aspect.

80 MACBETH

are metaphor and simile (see below). Imagery is the collective or repeated use of such imaginative or figurative presentations of things; it can be employed for all of the terms which refer to objects and qualities and which appeal to the senses and the feelings (see section on Imagery in Critical approaches)

metaphor a figure of speech in which a word or phrase is applied to an object or action that it does not denote literally in order to imply a resemblance. An example from *Macbeth*: 'He cannot buckle his distempered [unruly] cause / Within the belt of rule' (V.2.15–16)

pathos an experience that arouses feelings of pity, sorrow or sympathy

postmodernist a very vague term describing a variety of critical approaches united in challenging the idea that a word or a text can have a single, undisputed meaning. The author is denied any proprietorial or exclusive claim to the interpretation of his or her writing. All language is slippery and subject to a plurality of readings according to circumstances and the changing viewpoint of different readers

psychoanalytic a term describing critical approaches which are particularly interested in exploring the connections between conscious and unconscious elements in characters, the gaps between the revealed and the hidden in actions and language. The work of Sigmund Freud (1856–1939) inspired later critics to utilise and develop his theories of personality, desires and disguise in exploring how literature manifests the tensions in its creators and how it appeals to readers

rhetorical the ability to use language effectively

simile a figure of speech that compares two different things – usually using words such as 'like' and 'as'.

soliloquy a dramatic convention in which a character, unheard by other characters, thinks aloud about motives, feelings and intentions. The audience is given direct access through the soliloquy to the character's inner thoughts. In *Macbeth* the use of the soliloquy gives a sense of extraordinary depth to the main characters and provides the audience with a perspective on the characters not available in the public actions and words of the plays. Lady Macbeth's sleep-talking scene is a special development of the soliloquy

syntax the arrangement of words in their appropriate forms and proper order, in order to achieve meaning and particular effects and emphases

TIMELINE

WORLD EVENTS	SHAKESPEARE'S LIFE (DATES FOR PLAYS ARE APPROXIMATE)	LITERATURE AND THE ARTS
1040 Macbeth kills Duncan		
1057 Macbeth is killed		
1492 Christopher Columbus sails to America		
1534 Henry VIII breaks with Rome and declares himself head of the Church of England		**1513** Niccolò Machiavelli, *The Prince*
1556 Archbishop Thomas Cranmer burned at the stake		
1558 Elizabeth I accedes to throne		
1564 Galileo Galilei born; Michelangelo dies	**1564** Born in Stratford-upon-Avon	
1568 Mary Queen of Scots taken prisoner by Elizabeth I		**1565–7** English translation of Ovid's *Metamorphoses* by Arthur Golding
1570 Elizabeth I excommunicated by Pope Pius V		
1571 Battle of Lepanto		**1572** John Donne and Ben Jonson born
		1576 Erection of first specially built public theatres in London – the Theatre and the Curtain
1577 Francis Drake sets out on round the world voyage		**1577** Raphael Holinshed, *Chronicles of England, Scotland and Ireland* (reprinted in 1587)
1582 Outbreak of the plague in London	**1582** Marries Anne Hathaway	**1581** Barnabe Rich, *Farewell to the Military Profession*
1584 Walter Raleigh's sailors land in Virginia	**1583** Daughter, Susanna, is born	**1584** Reginald Scot, *The Discovery of Witchcraft*
1587 Execution of Mary Queen of Scots after implicated in plot to murder Elizabeth I	**1585** Twins, Hamnet and Judith, born	**1587** Christopher Marlowe, *Tamburlaine the Great*
1588 Spanish Armada defeated	*c.***1585–92** Moves to London	*c.***1589** Thomas Kyd, *The Spanish Tragedy* (first revenge tragedy)
1589 Accession of Henri IV to French throne	**late 1580s – early 1590s** Probably writes *1–3 Henry VI* and *Richard III*	**1590** Sir Philip Sidney, *Arcadia*; Edmund Spenser, *The Faerie Queene* (Books I–III)
	*c.***1590–5** Writes *King John*	
1592 Plague in London closes theatres	**1592** Writes *The Comedy of Errors*	**1592** Christopher Marlowe, *Doctor Faustus*
	1593 Writes *Titus Andronicus, The Taming of the Shrew*	
	1594 onwards Writes exclusively for the Lord Chamberlain's Men; writes *Two Gentlemen of Verona, Love's Labour's Lost, Richard II*	
	1595 Writes *Romeo and Juliet, A Midsummer Night's Dream*	
1596 Francis Drake perishes on expedition to West Indies	**1596** Hamnet dies; William granted coat of arms	

TASK 3

The violent descriptions and bleak settings enhance the Gothic tone of the play.

- Shakespeare wrote the play to be performed, not studied as a text. The Gothic setting evokes atmosphere and, in places, might frighten the audience when seen on stage.
- The Witches are not quite female and not male and are part of an excellent first scene. The thunder and lightning give the audience the right perception that the Witches are evil.
- Outside and inside castles, battlefields and the use of the supernatural are all part of the Gothic element in the play. They enhance the play by evoking excitement and mystery.

Shakespeare uses contrasting settings to build and sustain dramatic tension.

- The castle – with conspiracies in dark corners and murders – the setting of the heath with its thunder and lightning, the descriptions of the violent night and the deaths, all make good drama.

TASK 4

The murder of Duncan brought Macbeth great success.

- Macbeth became king after the murder of Duncan.
- He soon became unpopular and found the kingship unsatisfying.
- To retain the kingship, Macbeth felt he had to commit atrocities. He was not considered great or successful but a tyrant.

Macbeth immediately failed to find his kingship satisfying.

- Having murdered Duncan, Macbeth fails to say 'amen' (II.2.27). This suggests he has lost his peace.
- He cannot sleep soundly, which suggests he has a guilty conscience.
- His relationship with his wife declines and he plans to murder his friend Banquo.

TASK 5

Macbeth is foolish when he places his trust in the Witches' prophecy that **'none born of woman shall harm Macbeth'**.

- Macbeth interprets the original prophecies to his advantage – which proves to be foolish.
- He should have realised sooner that the Witches were **'juggling fiends'** (V.8.20).
- Macbeth should have taken Banquo's advice, that the Witches **'win us to our harm'** (I.3.123).

By Act IV Macbeth is desperate and he visits the Witches as a last resort.

- At this stage in the play, Macbeth feels that everything is spiralling out of control. He has seen Banquo's ghost and almost told the nobles that he was implicated in the murders. He has nothing to lose.
- He seeks reassurance, which he believes the Witches can give him.
- He wants to regain control of the situation.

MARK SCHEME

Use this page to assess your answer to the **Worked task**, provided on pages 96–7.

Aiming for an A grade? Fulfil all the criteria below and your answer should hit the mark.*

> **To what extent do you think Shakespeare presents life on earth as chaotic and diseased in *Macbeth*?**

A01

Articulate creative, informed and relevant responses to literary texts, using appropriate terminology and concepts, and coherent, accurate written expression.

- You make a range of clear, relevant points about chaos and disease.
- You write a balanced essay covering both positions – agreeing and disagreeing with the idea.
- You use a range of literary terms correctly, e.g. **dramatic irony**, **pathos**, **hamartia**.
- You write a clear introduction, outlining your thesis and provide a clear conclusion.
- You signpost and link your ideas about chaos and disease.

A02

Demonstrate detailed critical understanding in analysing the ways in which structure, form and language shape meanings in literary texts.

- You explain the techniques and methods Shakespeare uses to present chaos and disease and link them to the main themes of the text.
- You may discuss, for example, the ways in which Lady Macbeth's madness can be seen as a form of disease, acting as a symbol of her husband's rotten reign.
- You explain in detail how your examples affect meaning, e.g. the way in which Lady Macbeth's behaviour becomes more and more erratic at the end of the play, feeding off and contributing to the chaos on stage.

A03

Explore connections and comparisons between different literary texts, informed by interpretations of other readers.

- You make relevant links between the imagery of disease and immorality in Macbeth and another text, e.g. Wilde's *The Picture of Dorian Gray*.
- When appropriate, you compare the use of chaotic nature in the course of the play with the presentation of unruly or symbolic forms of nature in other text(s), e.g. the lashing wind and rain reflecting Heathcliff's tortured soul in *Wuthering Heights*.
- You incorporate and comment on critics' and/or audiences' views, e.g. James I's notion of the divine right of kings and how a regicide would disturb God's rightful ordering of the world.
- You assert your own independent view clearly.

A04

Demonstrate understanding of the significance and influence of the contexts in which literary texts are written and received.

You explain how relevant aspects of social, literary and historical contexts of *Macbeth* are significant when interpreting expressions of chaos and disease. For example, you may discuss:
- Literary context: biblical notions of divine order were core beliefs and the Bible a key text.
- Historical context: Life in Jacobean times was harder and more brutal perhaps producing more fatalistic attitudes to life on earth.
- Social context: Madness and disease were not understood in the same way as today making Lady Macbeth's behaviour a threat to social order.

This mark scheme gives you a broad indication of attainment, but check the specific mark scheme for your paper/task to ensure you know what to focus on.